OUT OF HER LEAGUE

KAPOW SERIES, BOOK #1

RENÉE DAHLIA

Out of Her League

Copyright © 2020 by Renée Dahlia

ISBN 978-0-6489626-0-1

All rights reserved.

No part of this book may be reproduced in any form or by any electronic or mechanical means, including information storage and retrieval systems, without written permission from the author, except for the use of brief quotations in a book review.

OUT OF HER LEAGUE

She is his greatest fan. He wants more than adoration…

JOEY MANANUI has had it all. The dizzying heights of a successful rugby league career, the lows of a career ended when he fractured his spine during a game. Now, three years after becoming a paraplegic, he has returned to success, thanks to the huge sums people pay to listen to his inspirational story. Only one thing is missing from his life, a partner who cares more about him than his fame.

ELLA TART is a massive fan of Joey Mananui. She has followed his story from his sensational debut through to his awful injury. When she books tickets to see him on the final night of his Leagues Club tour, she gets more than she bargained for. An incredible one night stand.

But when he arrives at her work a few days later, and her boss wants them to work together, Joey and Ella both have their own motivations for keeping their one night stand secret. They just need to keep their hands off each other…

Content Warnings
    Alcoholism, cancer, mention of suicide.

ABOUT THE AUTHOR

Renée Dahlia is an unabashed romance reader who loves feisty women and strong, clever men. Her books reflect this, with a sidenote of awkward humour. Renée has a science degree in physics. When not distracted by the characters fighting for attention in her brain, she works in the horse-racing industry doing data analysis and writing magazine articles. When she isn't reading or writing, Renée spends her time with her partner and four children, volunteers on the local cricket club committee, and is the Secretary of Romance Writers Australia.

ACKNOWLEDGMENTS

I acknowledge the Wangal people of the Eora Nation whose land this work was produced on. I pay my respects to Elders past and present.

Thank you to Ashfield for being a wonderful, welcoming, diverse community. To my cousin Hemaima, for listening to all my questions – it's been a long time since I lived in New Zealand, and your patience in helping me remember Māori language and culture is gratefully received. Kia ora. To Col Mackereth for sharing his fascinating life with me – the road rage story is inspired by one of our chats. To Kelly Huang for teaching me and my kids Mandarin and Cantonese.

For my gorgeous grandma, Doreen. Thank you for the Christmas story, and many other tales of madcap adventure. For Mr Cochrane. My year 4 teacher who gifted me a love of maths, and who is an amazing wheelchair rugby player.

1

"Mananui." Joey answered his phone in a flat tone. Why the fuck did people feel the need to call just before he went on stage? The flashing notification with his cousin and agent's name was the only reason he'd bothered to answer. Tonight marked the last event in his Leagues Club tour and his biggest audience to date. When the event sold out, they'd moved it from the local club to one of Sydney's biggest hotels and even with triple the original tickets, the sold out sticker had gone up again. He clamped down the churn in his stomach—audiences were all the same, regardless of size. Sure.

"Hey, cuz, I know it's the worst time, but I've got a great opportunity for you."

"Wiremu." Joey could wring his cousin's neck. This had better be worth the interruption to his routine. "What sort of thing?" He tried to infuse the sentence with as much disdain as possible.

"An advertising agency, they call themselves Kapow—"

Wiremu started, and Joey clenched his teeth. This couldn't possibly be urgent.

"—want you to be the face of a new campaign. Mate, this is huge."

"Later." Joey hung up on his cousin. He'd ask for forgiveness later when he wasn't trying to settle his stage nerves. No matter how often he spoke in public, it didn't get any easier. Joey shoved his phone into his jacket pocket and wheeled over to the elevator. He stabbed the down button with his middle finger. What in the hell was Wiremu thinking? He blew out a frustrated breath. The call had completely messed with his routine. Just what he didn't need before he had to go on stage. He pulled in a few deep breaths, like he used to when he had pre-game nerves. Confidence settled around him again and his pulse calmed.

When he'd broken his spine three years ago, his whole world had stopped. In an instant, one mistimed tackle had ended his career as one of rugby league's greatest players. Four Origin wins, a Dally M medal, an NRL premiership with his beloved Tigers, and an Australian cap. He'd hoped to play for a few more years, perhaps captain the Australian side, but everything changed in that split-second. He'd known immediately—from the sickening crack in the base of his back, even before he hit the ground—he'd never play another game. For the first year, all through the rehab, he'd grieved for his lost career, and he'd discovered which of his teammates were true friends. He'd used the insurance payout to create a house that worked for him, and when everyone assumed that he'd live off the remaining funds, his cousin Wiremu had created a lucrative new career for them both.

People wanted to hear his story, damned inspiration porn, but they paid ridiculous amounts of money for it. Unlike so many of his fellow players who had thought the big players salary would last forever. Now retired, they worked as bricklayers, scaffolders, and other physical jobs, every day slogging their butts off to earn a meagre income. He shouldn't have been so harsh with Wiremu—he was only doing his job—so he quickly flicked him a text.

Joey: Let's chat after the show

Wiremu: (thumbs up)

Life had an odd way of changing course, and he'd turned his injury into a huge opportunity. He could have been just like his teammates with a post-sport retirement of hard grind, not enjoying the gorgeous view over the Tasman Sea from his Coogee house. When a storm rolled in, grey and ominous, he loved to breathe in the energy of it, alive as it lashed his house. On long summer days, with the hot Australian sun glinting off the sea, he could relax with a beer on his deck, the heat slowly warming him.

He closed his eyes and let out a long breath. Yeah… He nodded. He could thrill this crowd of people who'd never know the gut busting joy of an Origin try, or the depth of despair when he knew he'd never feel his feet again. He'd talk, he'd listen to them cheer, and he'd get that same rush that his sport had given him. The lift doors opened, and he wheeled himself in. He enjoyed this life. The churn in his gut settled back to its usual pre-stage level, there but not overwhelming.

"Excuse me." A soft lilting voice came from the corner of the lift. It cut right through his frustration with Wiremu, and his hands loosened their grip on his chair. He looked up to see a petite woman with black hair pulled up into a sophisticated, tight bun. Her perfectly fitted sharp business suit emphasised her subtle curves. Only her shoes showed any personality; tall black heels with silver highlights that drew his eye to her narrow ankles and slim legs. Light glinted off the side of her head, drawing his attention to a rose gold ring that pierced the top of her ear. The odd placement intrigued him. It added a sense of playfulness to the precision of her clothing. He let his gaze roam over her tidy form, admiring the way her breasts curved with the tailored jacket. It was probably his overactive imagination, but he was sure that she shifted her shoulders slightly back under his perusal lifting her perfect, neat breasts towards him. His jaw slackened and he closed his mouth. A quiet scent of vanilla wafted past, washing away the tightness in his chest. Now his pulse raced for a different reason.

"Yeah?"

"Are you Joey Mananui?" She leaned towards him, a tint of pink on her cheeks. She imbibed his name with a breathless awe that was somehow fresher than the overt fandom others used when they spoke his name.

"Yes, and you are?" He heard the last vestiges of irritation in his voice and took a deep breath.

"Ella Tart." She bit her bottom lip, and her white teeth dug into the soft, pink flesh. "I know you are probably late to be on stage, I have a ticket, and I'm late too, but would you mind signing something for me?" Her words galloped out of her. He'd been doing this for too long. On every other fan, he found the admiration tiresome, but her zesty enthusiasm delighted him. And her name—her surname had to be fake—but he wanted it to be a promise. He wanted to whisper her name in her ear, to feel the shiver of pleasure in response. Sinful thoughts rushed in his brain, roaring like an excited crowd in his ears.

"What would you like me to write?" His voice deepened as she rustled in her bag. She looked up at him with her brown eyes glinting, and a smirk on her lips.

"For Ella. Love Joey." She laughed, a throaty sound that rumbled inside him. The self-depreciating joke, offered with a twinkle of humour flashing in her eyes, was precisely what he needed before he went on stage. He wanted her to laugh against his skin, to fulfil the promise in her voice as her mouth vibrated on him, her breath against his throat. His whole body pulled towards the attentiveness in her gaze. She slipped her hand into her bag and rummaged around.

"You know if women's clothes had better pockets, I wouldn't need this ridiculously oversized bag. And then I wouldn't carry around all this junk." She tilted her head and grinned at him.

"Your clothes don't have pockets?"

"No. And isn't it just the stupidest thing? I bet you have all sorts of pockets in that coat. Even secret special ones in the lining. And more in your shirt."

"Yeah. And even more in my pants." He laughed as she faux-scowled at his comment, but when her gaze dropped to his lap, the laugh stuck in his throat. Heat traversed his skin, and his heart started to gallop. A lifetime ago, he would have pulled her against him and taken advantage of his fame to kiss her. But life had taught him caution, to search for something real under this hum of lust in his veins. She pulled a pen out of her bag and held it out for him, a standard black ball point pen that spoke of a sensible nature at odds with her off the cuff charm. As he took the pen, his fingers brushed hers and a zing of electricity rushed up his arm and slammed into his chest. His hand tightened around the pen, as she thrust her hand back into her bag.

"I have some paper in here too. Just give me a moment." Her nose crinkled as she searched. He couldn't look away from her face, at the sudden concentration on her brow. Back in his playing days, he'd had strings of gorgeous women and a few men, each wanting a piece of his fame and he'd taken what they offered, but none of them had this natural joy that bubbled out of Ella. Or maybe it was simply because it'd been a while since anyone had enjoyed his company without a hesitation. One glance at his chair usually sent them scurrying away, yet Ella hadn't paid it any attention. She'd focused on him. No wonder he found her attractive beyond the tidy package of her body. He tensed, waiting for when the inevitable dismissal would come.

"Ah huh! Found it." She pulled out a scrap of paper with a flourish. The paper slipped from her fingers and floated in the air. She dropped to her knees and grasped the paper as it landed on the lift floor. She shifted her body to block him from seeing it, but he saw enough. He recognised that photo. It'd been in his debut season, over a decade ago, when some photographer had taken a photo of him walking out of the surf, saltwater glistening on his bare chest. He gulped as the headline flashed before his eyes.

GAME CHANGER: Meet NRL's newest, hottest star

He blinked. She'd kept it in her bag for more than ten years? She scrambled to her feet, and her skirt pulled tight across her heart-shaped bottom. He hadn't imagined that he could be so interested in just watching someone. They'd hardly even touched, just one brush of fingertips. She straightened, shoulders square, and stared defiantly at him. He grinned at the blush that painted her cheeks while she stuffed the old magazine cover back in her bag.

"I'd be happy to sign that for you," he said. She shook her head so hard that her hair loosened, leaving long black tendrils to frame her face, softening the business-like style. She stared at him with a defiant bold look in her eyes.

"Fine." She dug her hand into her bag but kept her eyes on him. He admired the way she didn't look away or hide, just embraced her embarrassment with a dare in her gaze.

"You've been a fan for a while then?" he asked.

"Of the Tigers? Yes, since I was a kid…" she said. He grinned as she deftly mentioned his team and avoided his question. She flicked her eyes down to her bag and handed him the magazine cover.

"What was it you said? To the bold girl in the lift?" he said, waving the pen. The roar in his ears changed to a quiet wind that whispered 'pick her' when she laughed out loud. The joyous noise burst out of her, filling the enclosed space in the lift with pure happiness.

She lifted one shoulder. "If that pleases you." Her words stroked his skin, making the hair on his lower belly stand up. *Oh, yeah, you please me.* Her blush deepened. He held out his hand and waggled his fingers for the paper. Her fingers brushed across his wrist, skimming his speeding pulse. He snatched his hand away as her touch sent a new shockwave of sensation along his skin. Before he could argue with himself, and decide against it, he autographed the front, then flipped the paper over and scribbled a quick note on the back.

Meet me after my talk. Room 3201.

A tiny nervous weight started to form in his stomach. She glanced at his message, then looked deep into his eyes, and grinned.

"Sounds like a plan. But if I do, I want the fake love note."

"Agreed." If she fucked with the same musical joy she had in her voice, he'd give her the bloody world. The lift dinged, and the doors slid open. He let his gaze roam over her, devour her. He nodded once, spun around, then rolled out to face his audience with a dorky grin on his face.

E lla sank against the lift wall and let out a shuddery breath. Had she just agreed to a one night stand with Joey fucking Mananui? Holy shit. She'd been in lust with him for more than ten years, ever since he debuted for her beloved Wests Tigers when she'd been just seventeen. And when he'd had his accident three years ago, she'd sobbed as if he'd been a close friend, refreshing the news on her phone endlessly for days in the vain hope that he'd be fine. Her breath raced as she rested the back of her head against the cool glass. A poster announcing his Leagues Club tour hung on the opposite wall of the lift, Joey's open, handsome face staring at her from his promotional photo. The doors slid shut. She shook out her hands. She preferred to take her pleasure on her terms, selecting partners for the sexual attributes—cleanliness, impersonal sex with great technique, guaranteed orgasms without any emotional risk.

Nothing like this. Not this heat of the moment, spontaneous madness. That low ebb of lust that simmered before tonight now roared to life. His power and confidence as his gaze took her in, those deep brown eyes, broad nose and full lips, so much more handsome in real life, up close with the air shimmering between them as he calmly assessed her. The chair didn't change his aura, didn't soften his appeal. How could it when his broad shoulders filled the space, his bare hands resting loosely on his wheels? His formal jacket covered his muscles, but her imagination and memory filled in the gaps. How many hours had she stared at photos of him? His broad chest, narrow waist, those little muscles over his hip bones... she swallowed. He had an athlete's body, strong, fit, and his arms, oh my, his arms. She could barely believe she'd just breathed the same air as him, had agreed to touch him. Her fingers still tingled minutes after he'd taken the pen from her grip.

When that magazine cover slipped out of her bag, a rush of embarrassed heat had flooded her cheeks. She rested her palms against them now, as the heat slowly subsided. Was it childish that she'd brought it tonight? The photo of him, bare chested with his brown skin glistening as the sea dripped off him, was more than just a keepsake. She'd been there that day at Coogee with Sal and a few other friends to watch the team train. A rare respite from school and work commitments. They'd stretched out in their bikinis on towels and giggled together as the Tigers had a training session in the surf. With the warm sun on her skin, and her fingers trailing through the sand beside her, she hadn't been able to take her eyes off Mananui as the waves crashed around his strong, muscular body. Whenever she went to the beach, the smell of saltwater, and fresh air always reminded her of that day. He'd walked right past her after that photo was taken, his bare feet less than a metre from her body. Her blood heated as she recalled how his gaze had roamed her body. That memory had crashed back when he'd done the same thing just now, his brown eyes darkening to the rich depths of soil kicked up by football boots in the rain.

Never in her life did she imagine that in only a couple of hours, her hands would be touching those broad shoulders, those biceps that she'd ogled so many times. How many times had she stood at their home ground and screamed his name as he ran down the sideline? Her fingers caressed her throat. God, she was hot and wet for him already. She ran her hand down her side, past her swollen breasts and along the lines of her jacket, skimming over her stomach, sending a shiver of pleasure along her backbone. One finger slid under her waistband, her breath shallow and fast. The lift door opened and she jerked her hands, slamming them together behind her back. Two old ladies entered.

"Are you alright, miss?"

"Yes, thank you," she said with a squeak. She caught a glimpse of her dishevelled hair and flushed cheeks in the mirror. She plucked out the pins holding it in, untwisted it from its tight bun, and dragged her fingers through her hair to smooth it out. She re-rolled it in shape, stabbing the pins back in, as the lift dinged again and the two ladies exited without words. As the doors slid shut, she heard them begin their gossip. What right had those old biddies to judge her? She worked hard, had done ever since she was fifteen. That awful year when her father, Baba, died in a car crash, leaving just her and Mama to survive together. Mama had fallen apart, grieving into a bottle, and Ella had to balance work and school to hold their life together. Work had become a habit, a way to control her destiny as Mama lost control. Sex was part of that control. She didn't chase mindless passion like her mother chased the buzz of alcohol. She controlled her desires.

With an angry puff of breath, she pushed away her problems. Screw everything. Ella deserved tonight. She'd splashed out on a ticket to watch Joey tonight, a present to herself, a reward for her recent promotion at Kapow Advertising. Her best friend Sal might say that she didn't know when to stop working, or how to have fun. Just look at her now. Tonight she would have fun, she would take everything Joey would give her. A fresh shiver of delight raced down her spine. Who the fuck cared about anything! She had a date tonight with her idol, and he was as courteous as he was hot.

2

Ella blinked as the lift doors opened to the top floor of the hotel. Joey's talk had been everything she'd hoped for, the highs of his league career, his bravery after his accident, and now she was about to meet him in his room. Her knees were weak as she tucked her phone in her pocket and walked slowly down the hallway to room 3201, her pace out of step with her rapid heartbeat. She paused outside his door, then leaned against the wall. She pulled out her phone again.

Ella: Hey Sal, can we chat?

Sal: Yeah. Are you ok, hon?

Ella: I think I'm about to do something silly. Was it ill-considered, or just wildly risky? She wasn't sure. She only knew that her heart galloped and her fingers trembled. With fear or anticipation?

Sal: Ok? Silly, as in spontaneous and fun. Or silly, as in Help?

Ella: I might have agreed to a one night stand.

Sal: As in fun, then. Do it! You could do with some fun in your life.

Ella: Hey, I have plenty of fun.

Sal: Lol. No, you have pre-arranged sex with men you've interviewed about their 'attributes'.

Ella: Still fun. Plus you know why I need control in my life.

Sal: Sure. But maybe it'll be good for you to take a risk for a change?

Ella: That's not helping.

Sal: Step outside your rules for once. No wonder you are nervous.

Ella: Rules are useful. Besides, she might be assuming too much. The air had been electric between her and Joey, and a couple of touches in the lift had sizzled, but he'd only said 'meet me' not 'fuck me'. Her thumb left little sweat smudges on her phone's screen.

Sal: Is he hot?

Ella: Oh yeah! … it's Joey Mananui.

Sal: That'd be why you're nervous. Holy shit, girlfriend! Ella swallowed. Sal had nailed the problem. They'd laughed about meeting him in real life over coffee last week, when Ella had mentioned she was going to hear him speak. She might be breaking her own rules about sex, but it was Joey. Her first ever fan crush hadn't faded.

Ella: Yeah. His speech tonight was amazing.

Sal: Do it. You'll regret it if you walk away. Thank fuck for friends. Sal always knew how to get to the heart of things. This could be enjoyed and put away in her memory, a keepsake. Her fingers tingled at the prospect of tracing his biceps, trailing her fingers over his strong shoulders, and feeling his short hair against her palms. She pushed herself away from the wall, sent Sal a thumbs up, put her phone away again, and knocked lightly. A murmured voice called out a few inarticulate words and she eased out a shallow breath. A moment later, the door opened to reveal Joey. He'd ditched his tie and jacket, and his linen shirt clung to his rock hard chest, emphasising his flat stomach. He rolled backwards to allow her inside, and she entered. The door swung closed behind her with a quiet snick.

"Hey, Ella, come in." Only a few simple words, yet they rumbled through her in welcome.

"Thanks." How could one word sound so breathy? She knew why, because every word in his speech tonight had built the anticipation for this moment, as his resonant deep-toned voice had wowed the audience. To hear her name in his baritone now sent a new thrill spinning inside her.

"Do you want a drink?" Joey rolled back into the wide lounge, with full length glass windows that gave an incredible view of Sydney at night. She bit her bottom lip and glanced around the penthouse hotel room. It struck her that she didn't have all the power in this transaction, that she was entering his turf. His rich, luxurious turf. No wonder her pulse tremored with nerves. Damn it. Remember what Sal said. No regrets.

"This place is amazing," she said, deliberately avoiding the question about alcohol. Between that and the glamour of the room, the flutter inside her grew. She swallowed away the nerves and tried to convince herself that he was just another guy, that he wasn't someone she'd admired for years. Usually she was the master of this type of encounter, believing that she worked hard, and therefore she deserved to take her pleasure where she wanted. And, oh boy, did she want to fuck Joey. She was damp for him already. It had only taken one glance at his handsome face as he spoke her name.

"I bet you get a million emails after your talks. I mean, I know the whole story, and yet it gave me chills when you talked—" She heard the babble of panic in her voice and sucked in a deep breath as he continued to stare at her. Hungrily or annoyed, she couldn't tell. The lights of Sydney harbour glowed behind him as she clenched the handle of her bag.

He winked lazily, with a cheeky smirk. "My agent deals with those."

"Oh." She clamped her other hand over her mouth, then let it fall slowly as his gaze raked over her. He rolled closer and stretched out his hands towards her.

"You don't have to be nervous around me."

"How can I not be nervous?" Her eyes darted around the room, "I mean, you are Joey Mananui, and I'm just …. me." The last word came out as a whisper. The tremble in her voice irritated her. She swallowed away the sticky burr in her throat, and glanced back at his eyes, crinkled with amusement.

"Hi, just me. I'm just me too." He grinned, and she shook her head unable to prevent a smile breaking out.

"You think I'm thinking too much." Shit, was she thinking too much? Hadn't she come here to enjoy herself?

His mouth quirked at the side. "You are female. Comes

with the territory."

Nervousness flipped into irritation and she hugged her bag against the flurry in her stomach. "And since you are all man – an important famous man at that - you think you can just smirk at my nerves."

"Your nerves?" He blinked once in exaggeration, still grinning. "Have we just time travelled back a hundred years or something?"

"Fuck," she whispered, then lifted her chin. "You know what I mean."

He chuckled. "Yeah."

Her arms relaxed, dropping to her sides again. "I guess you think I'm an idiot. I agree to come here, and now I'm all—"

"All what? Bothered?" His smile grew, his eyes glinting with teasing laughter. Yes, she was bothered—hot and bothered—by the look in his eye. She was used to being the instigator. In charge. His fame shifted the balance away from her, but it was the way he held himself with utter relaxed confidence that altered everything in his favour.

"There is no need to be afraid. Come and sit here." He gestured to his lap, and his gaze burned on her skin as if he knew that she would do as he'd asked, commanded. The assumption prickled at her, and she wanted to wrestle that power back.

"I'm not—" It was true, she wasn't scared, not of him. Only, perhaps, probably, of herself. She'd interviewed, as Sal called it, enough men that she knew the creepy wrong second-sense when she might not be safe. It was easier with other women, less risky. Joey gave her none of that sense of off-ness, only a good giddiness that made her pulse beat irregularly. She swallowed away the last vestige of doubt. This was the legendary Joey Mananui, she'd come here deliberately to revel in fandom. Time to choose to sit in his lap and kiss him. Sal's voice rang strong in her head. Do it. Take a chance. She could tell plenty about someone's technique, about whether they'd be selfish in bed or amazing, from a kiss. She'd dismissed many a potential partner after an ordinary kiss, and there was much less risk in kissing someone than ending up in their bed. God, she hoped he could kiss. As she stepped towards his chair to sit on his lap, he wrapped his huge hand around her hip and started to pull her towards him.

"Stop thinking, Ella."

She tried not to bristle at the command. "Hang on, let me put my bag down, and I'll sit down."

"Sure. It wouldn't be the best start if you walloped me with that gigantic thing," he said. She laughed, clean and clear as the warmth from his hand on her hip seeped through her clothes.

"We already discussed this. If I had pockets…" She threw the bag onto the table where it landed with a clunk.

"What have you got in there? Rocks?"

She grinned. "Oh, all sorts of useful stuff." A few lipsticks in different shades, spare tampons, an old school romance that she didn't have on her e-reader, the kind of clutter that was in every woman's bag because they didn't have pockets. She unbuttoned her jacket as she stood before him, her fingers fumbling on the buttons as he kept his gaze fixed on them.

"You'd need bloody big pockets to fit whatever made a dent in the table." His dark brown eyes twinkled and her shoulders relaxed as she slid onto his lap. The chair wheels made it slightly awkward, stopping her from sitting completely sideways. She had to twist to face him, one hand landing naturally on his strong shoulder, the other resting on her own knee. Before she could process the heat of his skin, or the way touching him made her nipples tighten, he captured her mouth, his hot lips seared her. She sighed into his mouth. Joey. What she'd wanted was a clinical kiss to determine his skill level. What she got was something completely different. An opportunity for more. Heat. Connection. His tongue probed deep, his taste filling her, dominating her senses with rich chocolate and salted caramel, a heady mix, one that promised dessert. The taste of desire. Sinful. Exquisite. Her imagination was a poor cousin to reality. Warm satisfaction—she was correct, he was more than good at this—filled her torso, mingling with the heat of desire that began where their lips connected, and raced down to her core. She slid one hand up his neck. His short hair was rough against her palm as she threaded her fingers against his scalp, and he groaned into her mouth. She reached up, placed her other hand on his hard chest, the linen of his shirt soft under her palm while his heat radiated through the fabric. His masculine scent, salty, rich, sharp, sent a tremor of anticipation skittering over her skin. She shifted so one hip pressed against his arousal, as he coaxed her senses with his tongue. Her body melted, that warm rush of desire making her boneless against him until she jerked away, breathless. She panted, only barely noticing that he also breathed heavily.

"Do I pass?" Only a man with supreme confidence could ask that question in this moment, in such a way that the only answer was Yes. Oh my god, yes. She could only nod. He'd blown her brains away with a kiss, tantalising her as she softened, wet between her thighs and ready for him. How good would he be! She should never have doubted her instincts. She'd known in the lift that this would be amazing and being correct grew the potential between them. A deep all-encompassing satisfaction, more than the physical, was possible with Joey. It ought to scare her, except it was so enticing. She slid her hand from his chest, trailing her fingers along his throat as he swallowed, her back twisting so her breasts pressed against his chest.

"Joey." She wriggled in his lap as she tried to get closer to him. He reached up and tucked an errant hair behind her ear.

"You didn't ask about my accident and how that might affect me." His matter-of-fact tone jerked her back to reality. She tilted her head, puzzled at the sudden change in topic.

"You can't spring questions like that on me with no warning." Ella inhaled sharply, "besides, I googled it on the way up here."

"What would we do without the internet?" He chuckled. He rested one hand on the middle of her back, and the other drifted from her cheek, down her neck, tracing the edge of her jacket. Sparks skittered across her skin, little bursts that almost distracted her from his question.

"Don't you want to know what I discovered?"

"Sure, you might have terrible Google skills." His deadpan expression made her blink.

"Hey, my google skills are—" Ella realised her error as a slow smile spread on his face, the corners of his eyes crinkling. "Oh, you tease. So, anyway, apparently, it all depends on the location of the injury as to how much sensation you have, but then, I figured that you wouldn't have invited me here if it didn't all, you know, work."

He nodded. "Yeah that sums it up. I can give you anything you desire."

"I want it all." She captured his lips, trying to demonstrate her keenness in her kiss, to connect with ardour. He growled into her mouth, producing a vibration and a sound she wanted to treasure. She clenched her fingers against his head, as he stroked his hand down her side and up under her jacket. He tightened his hand over her breast, and she gasped at the burst of pleasure that shot through her.

"Maybe we should move to the couch, so we have a bit more room," he said. She broke the kiss and noticed her knee wedged hard into the wheel of his chair. Oh. She'd been so lost in the kiss that she hadn't noticed. A sharp breath whooshed out, emptying her lungs, until she drew in a deeper breath and looked around the room, blinking. A seductive smile slowly grew as she spied a tall backed chair.

"I have a better plan." She stood up, using Joey's shoulders to help her, marched to the chair, grabbed it, and placed it against the wall.

"I like how you think." He rolled to the chair and lifted himself from one to the other, his arms bulging through his thin white linen shirt as he swung across. Her hands tingled, she had to touch those muscles. Now. And without that pesky shirt in the way.

She hitched her skirt up, not all the way, just enough that she heard his sudden intake of breath. Yes. This is the power she loved, someone at her mercy. She stepped across his lap.

"Like this?" she asked, keeping her legs straight as she stood across him. His mouth parted, and his gaze stayed low, transfixed by the promise between her legs. A promise that throbbed deep inside her with anticipation. She slid her hands up her sides, still yet to touch him. He growled, deep in his throat, and grabbed her hips, dragging her onto his lap. He pulled her tight against him, his whole body connecting with hers in a surge of sensation. His hard cock made a tent in his trousers, pressed against her skirt, stretched over her hips, creating a barrier of her making. She would choose when to close that final gap. Her hands dropped to rest on his shoulders, as he kissed her. This kiss, even hotter than the last threatened to scorch her. His touch and his cock, hard and strong against her stretched skirt, his mouth against hers. It all added to something better than anything she'd ever experienced. She wriggled to get closer. He grabbed her skirt in his fists, and tugged it up to her waist, exposing her completely. She tilted her hips, closing the final gap between them. His cock rubbed against her panties, only her lace and his trousers between them. She slid one hand down, the cool fabric of his shirt soft under her fingers, until she reached his waistband. She paused, even though every fibre in her body wanted to rush, to grasp him and have him, because she wanted to draw out this moment. To torture them both, to revel in this passion, to cement the memory in her brain of that one time she fucked her hero. She eased her hips backwards. He softened his grip on her waist, gave her the space she needed, while he kept up insistent pleasure of their kiss. She ran her thumb down the bulge in his trousers. He broke their kiss on a gasp. One that she replicated.

"No wonder they call you Big Joey." Her husky voice sounded like someone else, someone lost in passion. This wasn't the impersonal encounter that she thought she preferred. This might be better, much better.

"I thought that referred to the whole package," he said, lazily. She flicked open his pants, and his cock sprang free. She wrapped her fingers around the hot length, silky skin against her palm as she stroked him, so thick that her fingers didn't quite meet her thumb as she encircled him. A drop appeared on the broad head, and she brushed her thumb over it. Wet to match the wetness between her legs. A rumble of sound rushed from his throat. He buried his head against her neck, his stubble rough against her skin.

She whispered against his ear. "Whatever you call it, I'm impressed." She explored his length, taking her time with the hard, silky length, tracing each vein, wanting to remember every second of this encounter, before she lost her mind to the building tension. His teeth scraped against the tendons in her neck as his hands swept down her exposed legs. Rough calluses on his palms and fingers added to the building sensations. She stroked him tight with one hand, her other clutching at his skull, as his clever hands stroked broad circles on her inner thighs. Her legs trembled with need as her pulse raced, and heat seared her core.

"Closer. I need…" She begged for his touch. He smiled against her skin, trailing kisses along her neck, as his fingers swept oh, so near, once again.

"What do you need?" He kissed her jawline, as he taunted her. Ever decreasing circles, ever closer, but not near enough. Teasing her until her body begged for him. And finally, his mouth met hers again for a kiss that drank in her moans, incinerating her as he cupped her wet sex.

"Yes. Please." Her hips bucked and her hand loosened on his cock. He slid his fingers under the impossibly thin barrier of her lace panties, and finally, finally, touched her properly. She sucked his tongue, as he played, again almost giving her what she wanted. His thumb brushed her clit and she ignited. Heat coursed over her body in waves as he sunk a finger deep inside her. She couldn't think, could only move her mouth on his in the rhythm she needed. He responded, giving her exactly what she needed. Another finger. Deep inside. The base of his palm pressed against her clit and pushed her over the edge as she rubbed against him. Her orgasm ripped through her, wave after wave of pleasure, her body clamping around his fingers. She'd never been one for noisy unfettered sex, and yet she screamed his name, begging for more, until she collapsed, her head resting on his shoulder. His cock throbbed in her hand, promising more.

"There are condoms in the drawer over there." His deep voice filled with gravel, reverberating out from his chest as she lay against him. He slipped his fingers out of her, lightly playing with her panties, building the tension again. She slid her hand up his cock, then placed both hands on his chest. His muscles pulsed under her hands as she pushed herself up to stand. Her legs wobbled, weakened by desire, unwilling to take the necessary steps to grab protection.

"Take off your shirt." She commanded, impressed that her voice still worked. She straightened up, keeping her gaze firmly on his. His eyes darkened, until his pupils disappeared.

"Only if you take off yours."

She glanced down, shocked to see her suit jacket still on, her skirt bunched around her waist. She wriggled out of her jacket, flinging it towards the couch. She grabbed at the buttons of her shirt and undid them frantically. The activity allowed her legs to regain their strength, so she walked to the drawer he'd indicated, pulled it open and selected a condom. She turned to see his naked torso displayed for her. The inky swirl of a tattoo rounded one shoulder, with the ends curling down across his chest, as if reaching for his nipple. Her mouth watered, she wanted to run her tongue along the design, scrape her teeth on his nipple and see his muscles tighten for her. To see the bands in his forearms as he clung to her.

"Take off your g-string." Once again with power in his voice. Her eyes narrowed, not wanting to give in to his command, but knowing that she would do it anyway. "You know you want to."

She eased out a long breath as her heart clambered and leapt in her chest, beating strong against her breastbone. She did. Want to. She licked her dry lips, placed the edge of foiled condom packet between her teeth, and eased her panties down over her hips. She turned so her bottom faced him, slid the lacy g-string down her legs, heard the sharp intake of breath as she bent over, exposing herself fully to him. She slowed her movements as he groaned, that deep rumble hovering in the air. She carefully stepped out of her panties, one foot at a time, deliberately taking her time as she eased the skimpy fabric over her stilettos. His gaze felt hot on her skin as cool air swirled over her wet pussy.

"Come here to me." She straightened and turned to him. He had his cock in his hand, his dark eyes glued to her. It was the hottest thing she'd ever seen, and pleasure rushed into her core, heavy and strong. She straddled him again. The air shimmered with their mingled scent, his salty masculinity, and her musk. He reached for her mouth, plucked the condom from her lips, brushing his thumb across her lower lip. She shivered. He ripped the foil, and deftly rolled the condom over his length. She stepped forwards, across him, ready to be impaled. Wanting, throbbing with the need to have him inside her. The end of his cock met her entrance and she pressed down. He held her hips still, controlling her with such strength that it didn't matter that her knees had turned to jelly. He kept her poised above him, waiting, teasing her as his hands guided her movements. The head of his cock filled her entrance, a temptation.

"More. I want all of you," she cried out, desperation thickening her voice.

"Patience." He whispered against her cheek. "Patience."

His arms held her strong as she grabbed his shoulders and tried to lower herself, to sink onto him, but again he dipped her down, filling her just enough to let her know what he promised. And then he lifted her again, so the broad head of his cock waited at her entrance. The strength in his arms as he controlled her, even as she stood in a position of power, where she should control their speed, sent a wave of heat through her. She was ready to ignite.

"Fuck you, Joey. Give me everything." She bit his earlobe and he growled.

"As you wish." He slid her down, impaling her with his length, filling her, stretching her. She screamed, another orgasm ripped through her, her body shuddering as she clamped around him.

"God. Yes, Joey, Yes." She clutched his shoulders and used her legs to pump herself on his length. Together they moved up and down in the perfect rhythm. His fingers dug deep into her flesh on her hips, she'd be bruised tomorrow, and she revelled in it. She wanted his marks on her. Together they raced, working in unison gaining speed until they came together. He shouted her name while her world crashed around her, and there was only pure unadulterated pleasure coursing through her body. She slumped against him, annihilated by the pleasure, her fingers lazily tracing his bicep muscles, all the way down to his strong wrists. His pulse beat strong under her fingertips, a strength that she had captured for herself. Never before had she experienced this devastation, this vulnerability through strength. She'd always been in control, never begged for it, she'd always held something back for herself. He'd teased to the edge of need, taking her beyond herself, until she cried his name with want. Begging him for completion. This was a game changer. She had lost herself to desire for the first time. She should be scared, worried about what that meant. But all she could think was that she wanted it again.

3

"Fuck you, Joey. Give me everything." She had that wrong—she'd given him everything. Her molten heat around his length had sent sensation roaring through him. Thank fuck for that. He sent a prayer up to whatever gods had ensured he hadn't completely broken his nervous system, that he could still sustain an erection. The sensations were different to before, sharper in some ways, missing in others, not surprising really given the changes to his spinal column. She didn't seem to have noticed the lack of movement in his hips, since their position naturally lent itself to her controlling their pace. His arms ached with the effort of hiding his lack of function, even as he knew he was luckier than some. After months of rehabilitation, he'd finally had the mental space to worry about sex. Would he have to live forever with the memories of all those people who'd wanted to fuck a footy player? Any footy player, not him specifically, although he'd taken every opportunity. He'd tried to catalogue each of them, to retain each one in his mind, just in case. Then one ordinary day during physical therapy, a miracle happened. An erection. Completely uncontrolled, worse than his early teenage ones, but the gift of it had made him cry. An unbidden heat behind his eyes, a gratefulness to the goddess of luck. If he'd been hit on a different angle, or slightly higher, he wouldn't have this moment with Ella now. Or he would because sex didn't mean only penis in vagina, but it would have been different; without the burst of pleasure as he came inside her. He'd seen stars for fuck's sake!

Once he'd been able to leave the rehabilitation clinic, when he had the freedom of his chair and his own place, he'd paid a sex therapist. It had been worth every cent because she'd arrived at their appointments armed with medical knowledge. He'd had a few awkward encounters since then, none of them leading to any type of sex, and all of them making him ponder his future. Would he find someone who could look past his chair, past his fame, and see him? Ella had done the former, because of his fame, but regardless she had, unknowingly, given him a gift, thanks to her outright nature. It had taken all his strength and willpower to hold her, restrict her from surrounding him. He'd wanted to make her wait, to use her power to satisfy them both. He'd pulled her down his length so hard, using his arms to compensate for the lack of movement in his hips, he'd probably left bruises on her skin.

"Thank you." She stirred against him, lifting her head to look at him. He reached up and brushed a long strand of hair back from her face. Her once perfect swept up style, one that screamed corporate image, had come undone, and her straight black hair fell around her shoulders in an unkempt, delightfully natural fashion.

"I should be the one thanking you," he said. In the lift, he'd wanted to whisper 'Ella' in her ear, to feel her shiver with pleasure at the soft chant of her own name, and his breath against her earring. Instead, he'd shouted her name, loud, as his own body had exploded with bright flashes of gratifying bliss. He glanced down at her hips to see the bright red imprint of his hands on her skin.

"I hope you aren't too bruised tomorrow."

She flicked her gaze down, then stared at him with her nose wrinkled.

"Don't worry about me. I'll be fine." She stood up, helped him with the condom, and stepped away.

"I'll be more careful next time." Cool air washed over him, and he wanted to reach for her, to have her warmth against his chest again.

"Forget about it. I quite like the idea that I'll have a keepsake on my skin." Bravado coloured her voice as she looked out the window at the view.

"I don't want to hurt you." Joey whispered as she stood before him, her chest rising and falling. Her words might speak to an impersonal encounter, but the look in her eye before she'd turned away, and the tone of her voice told him that she also felt a deeper connection. Hopeful thinking, perhaps, but he couldn't stop the stray thought.

"Don't be ridiculous. I enjoyed this." She turned, spinning on her stilettoed feet, as she walked towards the bathroom with her skirt still bunched around her waist, giving him the perfect view of her bare legs and arse. He swallowed as his cock stirred. Shit, he should clean himself up first. A quick glance found his chair, it had rolled too far to reach from here, so he dropped to the floor, balancing on his arms, shifting himself quickly over to it. He swung back in, and rolled into the kitchen, before using a tea towel to clean himself. It wasn't ideal, but Ella was using the bathroom, and it seemed far too intimate to barge in. This might have been the best sex he'd had in a long time, easily the best since his accident, but that didn't mean he had any claim on her. This was just sex. Nothing else.

"It must be time for that beer. I'll grab one for you." Her softly feminine voice filled the room. He could only nod, unable to form words as she walked confidently towards him, draped in a hotel gown. Her black hair hung loose around her shoulders, against the stark white of the gown. He drew in a sharp breath and his cock responded like a rampant youth, an incredible reaction so soon after satiation, as he saw the gown hanging loose, undone, and her body completely nude underneath. From her throat, past the curves of her breasts, her belly button, and down to the dark hair of her pussy, clipped short, he had the perfect view of her. Her legs and feet were bare as she moved slowly, seductively, the gown swaying loose around her. He swallowed.

"Perhaps we should give the beer a miss." His voice croaked, his mouth dry. She smiled, reaching up to slide the gown back off her shoulders. It spread wider, giving him more of a view of her fantastic body. A flash of dark ink under her breast made his hands shift towards her.

"Or perhaps I'm thirsty." Her gaze fell to his lap, where

his cock stood up, once again demanding her attention. As she walked past him to the kitchen, she trailed her fingers over his shoulder. He spun his wheels to face her. She flicked the gown, and the fabric landed in his lap, dragging over his aching, hard cock as she stepped away. She opened the small hotel fridge door, then stood up holding a bottle of expensive craft beer and an apple juice.

"Even the drinks in the penthouse are better. Look at this, fresh squeezed juice, in a hotel fridge!" She set the two bottles on the bench, opened a drawer, then banged it closed.

"The opener is in the second drawer." So much for avoiding intimacy. Watching her in the kitchen, practically naked, in the simple act of popping a beer bottle had such a domestic feel to it. The hairs on his forearms stood up. He wanted this, and yet he didn't want it. Not at all. He liked his life. He liked the calm of his own house, the way he'd created it just for him, to work as he needed it to. He wasn't ready to share with anyone. He coughed. What the hell was he thinking? Share his house? This was just sex. Nothing more.

"Hurry up, will you?" He barked out the command roughly. So what if she was hot? So what if she obviously desired him. There were others that could provide this for him. Probably.

"Settle down." She handed him the beer with a roll of her eyes. "We have all night."

"Just one night though." He needed the boundary.

"Sure." She looked away, over his shoulder at the view,

before stepping past him. Her gown swirled in the air between them, a zephyr of dismissal that somehow also held sexual promise. The cool chill heated. He pushed the away unbidden notion that he could have more if he wanted, that he might want to share his life with someone. Someone brave, and hot, like Ella. He growled under his breath. He didn't need to share his life. He rolled his shoulders to ease the tension, turning his chair to follow her into the penthouse lounge. She stood by the large glass windows, staring out at the city lights, the white shine of the Opera House tiles reflecting on the dark sea. She lifted her juice to her lips and drank. His brain blanked at the sight, wanting to feel her lips on him. His cock throbbed as he watched her throat swallow. His own mouth watered. He placed his beer on the bench and wheeled towards her.

"Forget the drink. Join me on the couch." He tried to keep his voice light as he parked beside the couch and transferred himself across. He shifted, settled himself on a throw rug, stretching his arms along the back of the leather couch. Ella took another sip, her hand trembling a tiny amount as the bottle touched her lips. Was she nervous? He had the same twinge in his gut, as if this moment would mean more, if only they both let it. The depth of connection as she'd fucked him scared him a little. The way she'd understood how to pleasure him without him needing to explain made him yearn for more. She walked towards him, the white gown swinging around her legs, glimpses of her bare skin flashing as she moved with confidence and grace. She sat beside him, and as she crossed her legs, her gown slid off, leaving her nude from her belly downwards. He wanted to bury his face in that dark triangle at the top of her legs.

"Is this a traditional tattoo?" she said. He dragged his gaze up her body to meet hers, as she ran her fingers along his arm. Shocks of sensation sparked like electricity along his arm, making his pectoral muscles twitch. She traced the design, around each koru, every circle bringing her fingers closer to his neck and chest.

"Yes." His voice cracked, thick with desire. "It is based on the Māori legend of Maui slowing down the sun, bringing longer days and more light to the world. I chose it because I liked the idea that my sport entertains people, bringing light and joy to their lives."

"Is that how you've ended up on the speaking circuit? Still entertaining people, bringing inspiration to their lives?" She traced his tattoo with languid fingers as she spoke, tightening her grip on his shoulder as she reached her conclusion.

"Yeah." He paused, as she nailed the similarities between this job and his sport but stopped short of speaking about his accident and the aftermath. He didn't want to ruin this night with the pity, and the questions that always came with that topic. He slid his hand inside her loose gown, letting his fingers glide over her soft skin, across the base of her throat. She hummed as he spread his hand over her breast, and down to that hint of tattoo he'd seen earlier. He flicked the gown out of the way.

"What does it say?" He traced his fingers over the dark blue lines under her left breast.

"Jarndyce v Jarndyce."

"Are you a lawyer?" he asked, his fingers sliding along

the small words, tracing the shape of her breast. Her nipple pebbled under his palm and her breath sped up.

"Yes. The tattoo is an infamous case. It reminds me that lawyers always win." Her voice came out in a smoky whisper as she breathed out lightly against his shoulder, her lips almost touching him. "I remember when you got yours. The papers were full of pictures of you," she said softly, effectively shifting the focus back to her hand on his shoulders.

He smiled as her fingers splayed over his chest. "But you kept the one before the tattoo?" A coil of tension built in his gut. He wasn't that person anymore.

"Oh, that." A blush swept over her cheeks. "I was there that day, at the beach."

"And you've carried it around ever since?" It wouldn't surprise him. Fans did crazier things than that.

She laughed. "No. I brought it for tonight's conference because tonight was the second time we were in the same place together, even though you couldn't have known that. I guess it was on the off chance that you might sign it for me. But that seems pathetic now." She leaned closer, her bare body nestled against his side, and licked the ends of his tattoo. He groaned.

"There is nothing pathetic about you." He shifted, bringing their bodies closer together on the couch. "Tell me about your tattoo."

"I got it when I finally graduated. I had to study part time ... well, never mind why——"

He interrupted. "You shouldn't say that if you don't want people to ask."

"It's nothing much." She traced her fingers over his

hand, still resting on her breast. He raised his eyebrows, knowing that he could out-wait her. His injury had taught him the value of patience. She did that half-shrug that he'd already seen a few times.

"I had to support … myself, so I didn't have the time to study full time, not while also working full time. When I finally finished my degree, I gifted myself the tattoo."

"Let me guess. It refers to a long running case that eventually succeeded?"

She grinned. "It's from literature, actually. Charles Dickens wrote a book called Bleak House where the family sued each other, and eventually the entire estate was lost in lawyer's costs."

"Bloody lawyers, they always take their cut!"

"We end up with everything, that's what it means," she said. He laughed, his shoulders shaking, and her lips softened. His nostrils filled with the scent of her, of their mingled sex still lingering on her skin, of her own hints of vanilla. He closed the gap between them, cupping her face in his hands so he could tilt her lips towards him. A shot of tingling pleasure raced to his groin as they kissed. Her hands explored his chest, each touch on his sensitised skin burning him until he was alight with her. And all of this before the sweat of their previous encounter had dried. He couldn't move under her ministrations, not because of his old injury, but because he was transfixed by her. By the glow of her skin as she traced each abdominal muscle. His cock twitched, strained towards her, but she skirted it. Teasing him, as he had teased her. He growled into her mouth and grabbed her hand. He wrapped her delicate hand around his cock and stroked. Hard and fast. She matched him with her tongue, as his hunger grew.

"Suck me." He managed to croak.

She smiled against his cheek. "My pleasure."

Oh, no, it'll be all mine.

She threw off the hotel dressing gown and trailed kisses down his neck, to the base of his throat, where she licked along his collar bone and down, down to where he most wanted her mouth. She arched against him, her breasts pressed into him, as she slowly slid down him, her nipples tight buds as they dragged with an intense gloriousness over his skin until she knelt before him. Her hair splayed across his stomach, each muscle trembling with anticipation as her head covered his groin. He released her hand and threaded his fingers through her hair. Her tongue flicked out across the broad head of his cock. He gasped, clutching at her hair.

"Yes, tighter," she said. He pulled her hair and she moaned as her lips slid, wet and warm, over his cock. His mind blanked as sensation ruled. Her mouth sank over him, too slowly. He gripped her head controlling her movement. Every time he thought he'd been too rough, she moaned, and the noise reverberated around him. God. Holy fucking God. He pumped her head and she willingly took him deeper until he had to drag her off.

"I'm going to come in your mouth."

"That's fine."

"But I'd rather come in you." She gazed at him with wide brown eyes, her mouth open in a perfect o. She clambered to her feet, kissed him on the forehead.

"Don't move." Her command rang clear as she walked

away. Holy shit, his arms and chest were pinned in place by the sight of her, as she rose up before him completely naked. In a moment she returned, ripped open a foil, and rolled a condom onto his throbbing cock.

"Sit on my lap." He whispered, a throaty grunt that pleaded rather than commanded. She smiled with a sly knowing grin that sent a fresh wave of wondrous desire through to his pulsating heart. She turned to face away, her buttocks at his face level. He reached for her, grabbing her, pulling her down, as she lowered herself onto him. Before his accident, it had been his favourite position, to bend someone over a bed, or a table, any surface really, and pound into her, his hands sliding up her back and around onto her breasts, his breath on the back of her neck. It was his one regret, that he could no longer do this, yet somehow, Ella gifted him the same view. He hadn't needed to ask. Fucking hell. She held herself poised above him, his cock at her entrance, her back curved up and away from him with her hair loose over the long taut muscles of her spine. His fingers dug into her hips as he mastered the urge to come right there. He pulled her down in one big thrust.

"Joey." She screamed his name as she squeezed him tight. He focused on his hands, lifting her, sliding her up and down his length, his lungs panting for air in time with his arms. His biceps screamed with lactic acid, but all his focus was on his cock and the way she clenched him. She flicked her head, her long hair spraying across his chest and filling his desperate lungs with her apple and vanilla shampoo and the musk of their combined sweat. Her hands joined his— one on her hip, the other on her clit—and she climaxed as he jammed her down onto him, sending him as deep as possible. Her orgasm pulled his from deep inside him, all his overactive nerve endings exploding in pleasure, with an intensity that stole his breath. She shuddered as she relaxed back against his sweat slicked chest, and he slid his hands up to cradle her breasts as her head dropped back onto his shoulder.

"Thank you," he managed to whisper in her ear. The little gold ring at the top of her ear brushed against the top of his cheek, cool metal contrasting to the heat of their skin. He had no concept of how long they lay there together, time became an irrelevant concept as he soaked up every moment, every breath, to keep as a memory. Until she stood up, taking all her heat with her.

"I have to go now. Thanks for that. You were great." Her sudden change in tone from friendly and fun to dismissive and distant jerked him out of his sated state. Her hair whispered over his chest, one last time, before she walked away.

"Wait. Can I at least have your phone number?" Confusion made his blood run cold as she flung the hotel dressing gown around her and walked towards the table where her bag sat. She dug out her phone and swiped.

"What's your number? I'll call you and then you'll have my number," she said. He called out the numbers, irritated at her impersonal tone. His phone rang once from the kitchen bench where he'd left it, then stopped. She slung her bag over her shoulder and marched away. He closed his eyes and listened to the toilet flush, and the rustle of fabric as she got dressed.

"Thanks Joey." Ella called out just before his hotel room

door closed with a snick. How could she gift him the best sex, twice, the best he'd had in forever, then just walk away from him without a care? Had he read this whole connection wrong, and she'd just wanted to fuck a famous guy?

4

Ella cracked her neck as she turned away from her computer screen. The email this morning from their CEO Vince had been one line only.

'Clear your desks. Executive meeting at 1.30pm.'

She'd smashed her workload, getting Anna, Vince's PA, to bring her a sandwich and coffee at noon so she didn't have to leave her desk. This would be her first executive meeting. Years of hard work had finally paid off. First as a student, then in various firms until she'd got the job at Kapow Advertising last year. She had one line in the sand, and her body was it. She'd build her career with her brain, and it had been a hard fought battle to be seen as equal. Pleasure could be taken elsewhere, with people like Joey. She clamped down the delightful shiver of a memory that skimmed her collar bone when she thought about how bold she'd been, more than usual, forcing the power balance between her and Joey in her favour. A different shiver skirted the back of her neck, a rush of guilt that she'd walked away from him with such harsh words. She'd had to—to preserve the distance she required—it would have been too easy to lie there with him all night, chatting. She had no option but to leave. And quickly. The risk was too great. This, her career, was everything she wanted, a place where she could control every outcome. Not some unbidden emotional reaction, leaving her doomed to fall under the spell of her passions, lost to addiction like Mama. The moment she'd almost succumbed to feeling too close to him, resting her head against him in the aftermath of another glorious orgasm. She'd run away before contentment grabbed hold of her and owned her. It was a good thing it would only be a one-off, forever consigned to her memory.

Her phone dinged with the alarm she'd set. 1.25pm. Vince hated lateness with a passion, so she always set alarms for the rare meetings when he'd be there. Kapow's CEO was only young. If she had to guess he was in his early thirties, a couple of years older than her, yet he had a drive for success that exceeded anyone she knew. He'd built Kapow Advertising into the biggest ad firm in Australia, with most of the major brands on their client list. She knew the client list by heart, having written and approved all the contracts. She stood up, straightened her suit, grabbed her phone, notepad and pen, then marched down the hall from her office to the main meeting room.

Anna sat in the corner, laptop out to take the minutes, and Vince paced across the end of the room deep in a discussion on his phone. He wasn't the one talking, he only added cautious yesses and nos to the conversation, and when he spotted Ella, he held his hand around his throat and mocked scowled before smiling. She smiled back, hoping that her intimidating boss would see that she understood his joke about how utterly dull the person on the other end of the call was. If Joey was out of her league, Vince was in the stratosphere. Tall, hot-blooded, handsome as sin, the grandson of Italian migrants, Vince was a determined bachelor whose only love was his company. She slipped into a seat and nodded at each of the executive team as they entered the room. Stu, the strategic manager, who could talk the legs off a donkey. Muhit, the IT manager, so quiet and reserved that Ella found his silence judgemental and intimidating. It was probably unfair and more of a reflection on her than him. Muhit was just shy and he'd always been nice to her on the few occasions they'd had to talk. Craig, creative director, almost as driven as Vince, but with a crueller edge. Ross, finances, always hiding behind his glasses. And her, in-house legal, the only woman on the Exec team.

Precisely at 1.30pm, Vince ended his call, and turned to them. Ella leaned forward in her seat, her pen hovering above her notepad.

"Stu has an announcement." Vince didn't bother to say Hello, he simply launched right into business. "Stu, over to you."

"Thanks Vince. Welcome. Craig, Ross, Muhit, Ella." On her first day, Stu had stopped the rest of the team openly laughing at her surname, and she'd always be grateful for that. 'This is Ms Tart. She'll be our new in house legal, and I suggest that you wipe that smirk off your face over there in the cheap seats.' She'd been teased mercilessly in high school for her surname. If it wasn't for her pride in her heritage, and what the name stood for in Australia's history, she might have changed it the day she turned eighteen. No wonder her and Sal were such close friends, they'd survived the taunts together, her friend for being a lesbian, which, when combined with her own surname, had led to some wild accusations. It was all bullshit and they'd decided to embrace that rather than run from it. Friendship, sisterhood, and a shared interest in hot women—these things mattered more than some small-minded opinions.

"Next week, Kapow will have the privilege of announcing our new contract with a major sports brand. Thanks to our extensive client list, working with major sports brands across, Australia, Kapow has demonstrated our capability and will now head up all global advertising for the world's most renowned running shoe and clothing brand. As you know their branded tick is associated with major athletes around the world, and we've been tasked with taking their brand and making it more inclusive."

Ella's head jerked up at the news. This was massive. A global contract.

"I believe Kapow are best placed to take their story and make it bigger, more diverse, and more inclusive. We, as a team, need to generate a wider understanding of the issues facing the athletes who don't get the big coverage, athletes of colour, the women athletes, the disabled athletes, so we can push this brand's global reach into parts of the world they have yet to be seen. "Everyone is Welcome" is their new slogan, and our work will extend forward into the next round of Para-Olympics, the women's soccer World Cup, and other such sporting events. What are we doing to make the goal for our clients come to life? This question will require much thought in order to determine an answer, and I have to say, to frame that answer in a fashion that will deeply satisfy." Stu paused. Ella found herself nodding dutifully as his impassioned pleas.

"The announcement, Stu." Vince's voice cut the room, a lethal delivery at low volume.

Stu spread his arms in front of him, "I give you – the face of the "Everyone is Welcome" campaign. We have signed a VIP who will lead all our clients advertising in the lead up to these games."

Have we? Ella hadn't seen any contracts for this announcement. Before she could ponder who it might be, Stu stood up, and waved grandly towards the door.

"If you will, please, Anna?"

The PA stood up and opened the door. Ella's breath caught in her throat as she stared at…

"Joey Mananui. Dally M winner, and now, the face of Kapow's latest top end brand client." Stu's voice puffed with pride, but all Ella could think was fuck, fuck, fuck, and fuck. She had to work with him? Only a day after she'd bolted from his hotel room without explanation. This could get awkward quickly. Joey rolled into the room towards the front where Stu stood. Vince walked towards Joey and offered a handshake.

"Welcome Joey. Vince, CEO. It's a pleasure to have you on our team at Kapow."

"Thank you."

Stu followed Vince's lead, shaking Joey's hand and welcoming him in. He waved to the rest of the team, and everyone stood dutifully in line for their turn. Ella tapped her toes as she waited, dread pooling in her stomach. After what seemed like forever, the rest of the executive team had welcomed Joey, and now she stood in front of him. His lips curved in a secret smile as their hands touched, electricity jolting up her arm. He held her hand for a second longer than he ought to, tracing his forefinger lazily over her wrist, and she liked it more than she ought. She pulled her hand away, clenching and releasing it by her side as she retreated to her seat.

"Over to you, Joey." Stu waved to a space around the table, before walking to another seat.

"Thank you for this opportunity."

"We are pleased to have you on board. Of course we will showcase many other wonderful athletes in this campaign, but we'll be focusing on you. You bring a lot of gravitas to this campaign. You, Joey Mananui, are a big dog. You are the face of sporting disability in Sydney. Kapow can make you a global name." Stu shook his finger in the air as everyone nodded.

"Noted." Joey spoke with the same confidence that he'd shown in his speech the night they'd met. Heat blossomed on Ella's cheeks and she licked her lips, as she kept her gaze on her notepad.

"We are so excited to have you on board. Australians love you. You are a real inspiration to many. Everyone will be listening when you tell them about how Australia will lead the way in welcoming all athletes to the global stage," Stu said.

"Thank you. Again." Joey gave the impression he was

holding something back. The campaign would be a few photo-shoots, and a bit of filming of him doing sports stuff with other athletes, hardly anything to be stressed about. Ella tapped her pen against her notepad. How could he be upset with the concept when his entire inspirational talk the other night had been about his injury and rehabilitation? She was missing something. She shot him a quick glance to see if his eyes reflected his voice. His gaze held hers. Could no-one else feel the sparks of fire and ice that connected them? Joey leaned back in his chair, his hands behind his head, as Stu chuckled. Ella's fingers clenched her pen; better that than dream about caressing the underside of his arms, tracing the shape of the muscle from his elbows, the underside of his bicep where the skin would be softer. Her fingers tingled so much they almost hurt. Fuck, fuck, how was she going to work with him? And more importantly, how would she stay professional? She needed to prove to Vince and the rest of the Exec that she deserved this job because she was clever and worthy. The last thing she needed was a distraction like Joey. Stu continued to talk about their new client, and Ella scribbled notes as he rabbited on in that charming way of his.

"When do we intend to make this announcement public?" she asked. From the corner of her eye, she saw Joey lower his arms and nod at Stu's impassioned speech. She wanted to grin at the way everyone in the room had fallen under Stu's spell. His ability to work a room and have people agree with him was on par with Joey's ability to inspire an audience. The memory of that night, and now trying to deal with having him here in her workplace, distracting her with his knowing gaze, made her job so much more difficult.

"I take it you want a campaign launch with a bang." Craig spoke before Stu could answer and Vince waved his hand to stop anyone else talking.

"Stu will run the client liaison and create a timeline, Ella you need to sort out contracts, both with Joey and with our client asap, and Craig, get your team to put together some draft concept plans." With a simple command, Vince had ensured Ella would be stuck in a room with Joey for hours as they worked through the details of Kapow's standard contract.

"One thing, Vince. Will Mr Mananui be contracted to Kapow, or to our client with us as a liaison?" Her fingers tightened around her pen as she waited for Vince to decide how much time she would need to spend with Joey. Damn it.

"To us. Let's keep the terms broad so we can expand our relationship with Joey. I'm sure Stu will be able to utilise him for other clients too."

5

The flash of vulnerability across Ella's face as he'd made his entrance made Joey's chest tighten. It added to the emotional churn in his belly that had frolicked since their night together. She'd seen his chair, and rather than dismiss him, she'd dismissed the chair as a problem. Not only that, she'd cleverly found two different ways to fuck him that had taken his physical limitations into account while also fulfilling one of his deepest fantasies. And all by instinct. Seeing her seated in the board room added a whole different dimension to this job. Now they had to work together. He'd listened carefully to each introduction from the team, trying to figure out how to place her. He'd never forget she was a lawyer, her tattoo's placement forever in his memory, although he'd assumed something completely different to an advertising agency.

"I have to meet the Premier. Keep me up to date on your progress." The CEO of this joint stood up, shook Joey's hand once more and left the room. What a way to run a business, to hand an idea to this collection of people without discussion of budget! But then, what would a league player know about advertising? Maybe this behaviour was normal.

"What now? Do you want photos or something?" Joey asked. He kept his gaze on Ella. Her eyes widened and she shook her head at him as if to say *Pretend we don't know each other*.

"Details, details. We will get to those soon. Today is about the in-house announcement and a discussion on how we will frame that announcement in the media. How about we take a short break, a half-time breather?" Stu waved his hands expansively. Joey couldn't take his eyes off Ella as she pretended not to see him. Joey's chest squeezed at the irony, as he simultaneously craved her, wanted to help her, and was annoyed by the way she'd bolted like a scared rabbit after fucking him senseless. It would be a dick move to gain petty payback by mentioning that they already knew each other. He clenched his teeth together. There had to be more to the story, and he wouldn't find out by being an asshole to her.

"Great team meeting and strong announcement. As Vince says, the ball is in your court now Stu. Let me know when you need my creative team on board," Craig pushed back his chair, nodded to the room, and started to leave.

"Now. We need them now. I'll get Anna to drop off the brief from the client on your desk." There was a political undertone in the way Stu and Craig talked to each other, both of them harsher than they'd been while the boss was in the room. The last couple of years had taught Joey a lot about reading people.

"I also have work to do," Ross said, and while the other

guy, Muhit, only nodded in agreement and left. The dismissal shouldn't have bothered him, and he realised with a start that it was the way they all dismissed Ella that rubbed him the wrong way.

"Right, then. Anna, perhaps note the meeting closed. Could you duck out now? Also, can you grab the client information and throw it all on Ella's desk? They are on my desk." Stu dismissed the young woman who was presumably a secretary of some sort, leaving just the three of them in the room.

"Stu. Some heads up on this issue would have been preferred." Ella's voice became tight, pinched.

"What do you mean?" Stu's open expression had to be faked. Even Joey could see the problem with announcing this to the team before they had signed any contracts.

"Isn't it jumping the gun a little to announce a big new client to the team before a contract has been outlined. I haven't even seen a basic deal sheet on this issue. What is to stop the new client—or Mr Mananui—walking away from this before we've even started."

"They won't. Trust me."

"Why? Because you are the Strategic Manager? That's not enough. We need to lock this deal down on paper before we commit dollars to it."

"You are our in-house lawyer, you are the right person to ensure that all the legal requirements and what-not are sorted out."

Ella's nostrils flared, and she laid her pen down, neatly against her notepad. "It's rather difficult to do that when I'm not informed. All I'm saying is that we proceed with caution until those details are completed. We are both equal of the org chart. I should have been told."

Joey nearly smiled at the sudden understanding. Ella's temper came from being the only woman with any power in the room. Well, that must be a pretty tough place to be, no wonder she needed to be forceful to be heard. Her terse mannerisms suddenly made sense, and he relaxed. To leap automatically to jealousy showed how much the night with her had affected him.

"Vince didn't want the rest of the exec team to know until we'd nailed down the deal with the client. I'll forward you all the communications and you'll see that we have a—"

"Verbal contract." Ella tapped her pen on her notepad and lowered her gaze. "My apologies, of course, you are right."

Stu smiled expansively at her apology, apparently not seeing how Ella's jaw tightened. Joey was amazed at how Ella managed to navigate the underlying assumption of her place in the room, and he really wanted to know what she hadn't said. He completely understood the way she balanced wanting to be heard with the way the world stereotyped her before she could prove herself.

"Great. You sort out the details and once we have approval from our client before we can launch their new branding with full fanfare. I'll organise a photographer for the promotional photos with Joey, and by then Craig's team will have the nuts and bolts of the campaign ready to launch." Stu waved his hands demonstratively.

"Will they want naked torso photos?" asked Joey, purely

so he could see Ella blush. She rewarded him with a visible shiver, her face glowing red.

"I doubt that will be necessary, although the photographer will have their own ideas. I'll need at least three weeks to get that set up, so that would be your working timetable." Stu shook Joey's hand heartily, then paced out of the room, leaving Joey with only the board room table between him and Ella. She leapt to her feet, gathered up her belongings and held the door open for him.

Joey rolled towards her, pausing beside her. "I'm glad that's done with. I had no idea you worked for Kapow when I accepted this job."

"It's not a problem," she said with a slight shrug.

"Are you sure?"

"I rephrase. It won't be a problem if you keep your lewd comments away from work."

Joey grinned. "Lewd? You must know I only said that to get you to relax. Is it always that long winded and intense? How they get anything achieved if they all talk as much as he does?"

"Are you kidding? That was succinct for Stu, not even close to the longest meeting I've been in." She sounded resigned. Joey chuckled as he rolled beside her along the broad corridor.

"He's left you with a decent amount of work for all his talk."

"Look." She paused then spun on her skinny high heels to face him. "I don't care about the amount of work. It's work, that's normal. What I can't believe is your ridiculous comment about the photos, and the way you shook my hand like that at the start of the meeting. Oh my God, Joey, I'm trying to be professional, especially as the only woman on the exec team, and you goddamn caress me in front of my colleagues. Seriously." She sighed after berating him. His gaze dropped to her hands, all this talk of caressing had his own skin heated with memories. He wanted more of her delicious body, neatly tucked away in another business suit that emphasised her subtle curves.

"You can't have it both ways. Sex on tap when you want, then nothing when you can't deal anymore." He really wanted to know why she'd fled the other night. She tucked an errant hair behind her ear, and his hands flushed with heat. He needed to thread his fingers through her hair again as her lips covered his cock, to tug the long black strands until she groaned in that delightful mix of pain and pleasure. The knowledge that she had begged him to do it, the notion that their wants and needs met in the same place, made heat flood his face.

"I don't want both. Look, I've only just made the exec team. I can't have them thinking that I'll flirt with all our clients."

"Were you flirting?" He grinned as he teased her.

"I must remain professional, that's all." She exhaled, the pink on her cheeks fading as she stared at him. A frown flashed on her brow. "Are you feeling okay? You have a little colour in your cheeks?" She lowered her tone to a whisper and pressed her cool hand to his forehead. He cleared his throat as her touch seared him, oddly tender and caring as he fantasized about her touch in a totally different way, sending shards of desire over his skin. No wonder she thought he was flushed. For all her talk of professionalism, she appeared to be just as drawn to him as he was to her.

"Yes." He glanced up at her brown eyes, her black hair neatly pulled back into that sharp bun, except for one escaping strand that hung down her cheek and his fingers twitched. It took all his control not to reach up and untwist her hair so the rest of it fell over his hands.

"Your head is cool enough."

"I don't have a fever, if that's what you are thinking." He gave in to the need to touch her. He reached up and tucked that strand behind her ear, brushing past her earring, and letting the silky hair slid between his fingertips. Her soft vanilla scent lingered in the air as his senses focused solely on her.

"Should we go out for a drink?" he asked.

"No. I'd rather sort out this contract in my office." Only a slight twitch at the corner of her mouth gave any hint to hesitation, her voice doing a good job at sounding snarky. He kept his gaze on her, wondering if she deliberately made herself sound tougher when she was anxious. That aligned with her behaviour during the meeting.

"Your office? No. It's a beautiful day in the world's greatest city. Bring your contracts with you and we'll talk about them over a beer." His lips stretched into a smile. Light glinted off her earring as she tilted her head and considered him.

"Fine. As you say, it's a lovely afternoon. How about the bar out the front of the Opera House? It's a lovely after-noon." She repeated herself and the hint of nerves tugged at him. It made it much easier to have the necessary annoying conversation with her if they were both unsettled.

"I'd prefer Quay View, you know the bar that overlooks Circular Quay station. The view over the Quay is gorgeous from up there." He'd suggested a bar because he wanted to push her out of her comfort zone. If he could get her away from work, maybe she'd relax enough to explain why she bolted away from him. Damn his curiosity. He shouldn't yearn for her this much, not after the way she ended their one night stand.

"I guess that's why they called it Quay View. It makes no difference to me," she said. He heard a hint of something … disappointment, perhaps … in her voice.

"It makes a difference to me. The opera house might be iconic, but it was built before disability regulations came in." He wouldn't normally bother to explain or make such an allowance, preferring to leave people to work it out for themselves. It wasn't his job to teach people how the world worked for him, except she had previously looked past his chair as a problem, which put her into a unique category. Perhaps he imagined the disappointment in her tone.

"Does that mean you can't even get in there? Surely that's against the law. I can talk to someone." Warmth settled on his shoulders as she raged on his behalf, rather than dismiss his concerns.

"No, they have been retro-fitted, but it's awkward." Normal wheelchair access routes took extra time to navigate, at least compared to the standard entrances, but retro-fitted ones were the worst for the convoluted path they often took through a building.

"There are so many great options in the city, why go to one that has unfriendly access?" She did that half-shrug he was becoming familiar with; the one that looked like she was trying not to care too much.

"My car is in the basement carpark. Come down the lift with me, and we can drive there," he said. Her straightforward understanding and acceptance shouldn't matter this much. If only it wasn't a unique experience.

"Cool." She pushed the lift button then stepped through as the doors opened. He should have been annoyed that she went first, often that made him feel overlooked, down here at everyone's waist level. With her, a warm rush of chivalry filled his veins. The lift doors slipped closed behind him. He glanced up. Her cheeks glowed pink. He swallowed as his body recognised the shade even before his brain had registered it, not an embarrassed colour, but the colour of desire that he'd already seen on her.

"We've done this before—"

"Déjà vu." She spoke at the same time, her gaze locked on his. She bit her bottom lip, leaving a little mark that he wanted to kiss, to soothe. Before he could reach for her, the lift dinged, and they'd traversed the two floors down to the basement. Damn these fast lifts. He chuckled in wonderment. Who would have thought he'd curse a lift, simply so he could slow it down to spend more time with Ella?

He rolled out of the doors, pointing to his car. "It's that green one over there, the Mustang."

"It's quite an expensive car."

Joey grinned. "What can I say? People pay good money to listen to me." His chest expanded as he glanced sideways at her. He wanted to impress her, to fulfil the yearning in him for recognition that he retained his masculine power. "Come and check it out. I love the way it works."

"You don't seem like the type to waste money on a frivolous attention seeker like that." The chastise in her voice was ruined by her smile.

"You aren't impressed?" He smiled. "The set-up is super impressive."

She tilted her head and winked. "Should I be impressed? You aren't using the car to compensate for lack of size." She lowered her gaze to his lap, held it for a second, then smirked at him. A laugh burst out of him, a surprised punch as her eyes danced in delight at his response. Ahh, that's why he desperately wanted to understand why she ran. There was some reason and it wasn't about the fucking incredible sex they'd had. Suddenly, the two steps she stood away from him was too far.

"Kiss me." He hoped she'd say yes. He didn't expect her to agree so suddenly. She pounced, cat-like, elegant and gentle, into his lap, her soft skin a marvel of contrast against his rougher cheek as she offered her face up towards him. Her hands devoured him, tracing up his arms, gliding over his shoulders, sliding up his neck. His mouth found hers. He hissed as they connected, tongues and teeth clashing in a riot of sensation. Desire soared in his veins, as she held nothing back, even her eyes burned, flared as her dark brown irises glowed, the same way the edge of a campfire glowed, mixing night and heat. He drew in a deep breath, her scent flooding his nostrils, overwhelming him, making the dull smell of dust and old engine oil of the carpark fade into the distance. She shifted in his lap, slinking closer, and his chair rolled a fraction. He flicked on the brake, to free up his hands. He slid his hands under her jacket, traced her curves from her waistband up her side until her cupped her breasts.

"Damn you, Joey." She breathed out. He chuckled against her lips, and she responded, once more taking them to another plane of passion, and he forgot to ask her why she'd rushed off. Her fingers pressed into his skull, the pressure point sending a wave of heat rushing down his arms. She shifted slightly, so his hands ended squashed between her breasts and his chest.

"Come to bed with me."

She lifted her head, gazing wildly, unfocused around them, and gasped. The garage reappeared in his vision. She coughed. "Holy hell. You'll be the end of me."

"If it makes you feel better, I'd forgotten we were here too." He smiled ruefully, as she pushed herself to her feet.

"Anyone from work could have seen!"

"Maybe we should skip the drink?" He kept to his statement, using his invitation to distract her from the rising panic in her eyes. Only a few moments ago, she'd told him off for touching her at work, and he could see her brain whizzing at the prospect that someone might have seen them. Kissing. In the office garage.

"Your place?" The note of caution in her voice made him pause. He didn't want her to agree just because they'd near set the garage on fire with just a kiss. Or because she wanted to get away from her colleagues.

"You don't have to say yes." Joey ran his hand through

his short hair as she tugged at her jacket. She took a moment to button herself up, then stared at him with her business face painted back on. He missed her when she closed down and kept herself hidden from him.

"Joey." She must have heard the tension in her voice as she squared her shoulders and sucked in a deep breath. He tried not to drop his gaze to her breasts, to see them lift and fall as she breathed, but he found himself staring anyway. He shook his head and lifted his gaze back to her eyes.

"Ella, there is something worthwhile between us. Tell me you don't feel that?"

"That's just your cock." She shrugged dismissively. He held his hands out in front of him.

"You wound me." His irreverence had the right impact, and she laughed.

"I doubt that. Besides, you are a big boy, you don't need me to validate you."

"No. But I would like to have a quiet drink with you." *And explore you slowly.* Phew, at least he hadn't said that out loud. Her face flushed, a delightful wash of pink on her cheeks, so maybe she'd seen the sentiment in his eyes anyway.

"Damn you. I should head to the office, to do get this task started. Vince expects a certain standard, and here you are, tempting me into taking the afternoon off work."

"I don't see the problem."

"Some of us have to work for a living."

"Virtually everyone in the world works for the living, in one form or another. Most of them will take time for fun too."

She shook her head, and he thought she would walk away, but she lifted her gaze to his and smiled. "This is a terrible idea."

"You'd rather be stuck in your little office, just you, a computer, and piles of paper, than with me at the hottest bar in town, enjoying yourself as you achieve the same amount of work?"

She sighed, a full body sigh that made him burn with curiosity. "There is more to life—"

"—than work. I know, that's what I said."

"I was going to say, than frivolous fun." She crossed her arms under her breasts, right where that damned tattoo was hiding under her clothes.

"Fun is important too. Come along, have some fun with me." He hoped he didn't sound too desperate.

"I have plenty of fun." Her voice hit all the defensive notes, her nostrils flared and pink blotches marred her cheeks. There was definitely a story to be unwrapped here. He swallowed, he wanted to do a more physical type of unwrapping of her first.

"Fine. If it's such a problem, you can take the lift back to your office. You work, and I'll pretend that I don't mind being kissed and dismissed." He'd meant it as a joke, however, truth sang in his words.

She stepped back, rubbing below her eyes. "One drink. I'm not heartless, you know." He clenched his teeth to prevent a satisfied smile. Yes!

6

Would she ever be free from this need to control everything? There was so much more she could have said in that meeting if she was one of the blokes, but the old bitterness of her own struggles to succeed prevented her from speaking out. She didn't need to muscle into every conversation, just to prove her value. Ella watched Joey as he opened the driver's door of his muscle car and transferred himself in. He drove the ultimate sports guy car, it probably had a loud engine too, but she was the real stereotype. The daughter of an addicted mother and a dead father. No wonder she wanted to control everything in her life, to work her butt off in the vain hope of success, whatever that meant. She wouldn't be like her mother, who dropped every-thing for her next drink, for the fun of the chase, for passion. The rapid increase in her heart rate must be due to Joey's continual mention of a drink, not the way the air crackled with heat between them.

"Hey, are you coming?" Joey leaned out of the car, a

relaxed smile on his face. His chair had magically disappeared. She rolled her eyes at herself; he'd obviously put it somewhere in the car while she'd been staring at the back wall worrying about everything. Thinking about it wouldn't change it, so yeah, maybe she should take Sal's annoying life advice and have some fun. And she could do it without touching a drop of the evil liquid that had ruined Mama's life. Joey didn't mean anything by it. He wouldn't have said it if he'd known. Probably?

"Yeah." She'd often felt this tug—to abandon her responsibilities and follow the easy path, the fun path, but never before had she been tempted as Joey tempted her. His kisses made her forget. Forget what drove her to success, forget that she wanted a calm, controlled life where she wouldn't have to walk on eggshells wondering what the next day brought. She'd created this life, leaving home as soon as she could. She paid a nurse to visit Mama once a week and sent money that was probably wasted on alcohol. That choice was Mama's responsibility, not a reflection on her own life. Why did going to a bar in the afternoon feel like everything might change?

"Come on then. Check out my car." His voice snapped her out of her introspection. She slid into the front passenger seat and couldn't hold back a grin at the enthusiasm on Joey's face.

"How does it work?"

"It has this hand control that does the accelerate and brake." He pointed to a knob that stuck out behind the steering wheel. She leaned across him to peer around the wheel to see it properly. He rested his left hand on her shoulder, a patch of heat seeping through her jacket that relaxed the tension in her muscles.

"What do you mean accelerate and brake? Isn't that confusing?"

"Nah. It's kind of like flying a plane—"

"Because everyone knows how to do that!" She rolled her eyes, and her grin grew despite her internal worries.

"Yeah, okay. But you've seen planes at the movies, and they have that big handle for speed, right?"

"Yes?"

"This works sort of the same way. You pull the handle towards you to go faster and push it away to brake."

"Oh, how clever. It's so simple." She leaned closer, tucking her head under his chin to see it better. It looked like a boring round stick, but she used it as an excuse to sidle closer to him.

"Cool, huh." His breath whispered over her, little zephyrs tingling the roots of her hair.

"I'd be worried that I'd still try to press the foot brake in an emergency."

"Look, that's a concern. I'd been driving for a decade before my accident, and as soon as I could get out of hospital, I wanted to drive again. But wouldn't my brain want to hit the foot brake automatically?"

She gasped. How scary! Joey slipped his fingers under the collar of her jacket, little prickles of heat against her skin.

"I needn't have worried. It's just practice and will power. It soon comes naturally."

"Right, so you remodel the pathways in your brain?"

"That's what the geeks say." His laugh rumbled against her body as she rested on his chest.

"And does the rest work the same way?"

"You mean the steering wheel, and shit? Yeah. It's the same." His thumb traced circles on the back of her neck, and she closed her eyes to drink in the sensation and his welcoming aroma. A long slow sigh seeped out as he pressed his thumb against the tight muscle at the base on her skull.

"You like that?" His voice deepened, the gravel combined with his touch to give her gooseflesh and tighten her nipples.

"You know I do." She wanted to rub her body all over him, but the steering wheel dug into her shoulder, so she reluctantly straightened and sat back in her own seat. His hand loosened, trailed across her shoulder and down her arm, to rest near her elbow. She twisted to face him, to see his brown eyes darken with desire with an intensity that tore at her heart. Part of her wanted to embrace the potential in the emotional pull, but a larger part screamed in her ears to run far, far away.

"Shall I show you what it can do?" His fingers had slid down to her hand, and his large palm covered her hand, adding to the sense that she would lose control, lose herself and disappear. Tiny voices in her brain argued—relax, you deserve this attention—no, run far away—until she snatched her hand back and crossed her arms.

"The car?"

"Yes, the car. You already know what the rest of me can do!" Crinkles at the edges of his eyes marked his amusement and he glanced unsubtly to his lap then stared into her eyes.

"Is everything about sex with you?" She grinned to show that she meant it as a joke, but the smile disappeared when his face shut down.

"Perhaps I should ask the same question of you." One eyebrow raised as he stared intently at her. Her teeth clenched as she struggled to hold his gaze. She breathed in slowly, then eased it out between her pinched lips.

"It was a one night stand. It's basically the deal," she said, eventually. She didn't know how many minutes had passed, probably only a few seconds, but the strength in his gaze and his question made time slow so each rapid heart-beat took forever.

His eyes widened a fraction, then narrowed. "You didn't have to bolt off like that."

"I, ahh—" How could she explain? "—it's not you."

"Come on now. That is the weakest answer." That eyebrow raised even higher, his lip snarled with sarcasm. Her lungs rose and fell quickly as she scrambled for an answer that would keep her detached. In control. She'd been trying to stop herself get hurt and realising that she'd hurt him in the process did nothing to calm the ridiculous thump in her chest. Crap. She owed him an apology but it stuck in her throat.

"I'll explain once we've sorted out your contract. Show me what this car can do." She rubbed the back of her neck as he held her gaze. She looked away, bowing her head. The engine leapt to life and she couldn't help glance at Joey. He twisted as he reversed out of the parking spot, then the Mustang roared as he drove out of the garage, up the ramp, and onto the road. Under different circumstances, she'd love this. She cleared her throat. Why shouldn't she love it anyway? The questions could wait, so she tried to ignore the growing lump in her gut. They would come regardless, stressing about it wouldn't change anything. Focusing on the right wording for an apology would be a better spend of her time than stressing about whatever he might ask her.

They'd been driving for five minutes before she felt ready to glance at him again. His hands were relaxed, his left one on the steering wheel, the other on his special stick.

"You love this car." Her intended question came out as a statement.

"Yeah. It's freedom, you know."

"What do you mean?" Curiosity won over stubbornness.

"When I'm in the car, I'm just like everyone else on the road. No one sees the chair, no one judges, I can move without being stared at."

"That's just because you are famous." She knew the truth in his words, but she couldn't help but try to deflect away from the emotion in his voice. A rough laugh burst out of him.

"Yeah, I'm sure it's that." He paused. "It's not that. I know how people used to stare at me when I was famous. They stare differently now."

"I'm sorry." She didn't know what else to say. Her foot jiggled and she pressed her heel into the floor of the car.

"It's not your fault. It's not anyone's fault."

A million questions rushed in her brain, but none of them were appropriate. She didn't want to be curious because she shouldn't want to know more about him. Keep him safely at a distance. She needed to apologise for running away, that's why she was still here. Mostly. The pull of chemistry between them made it easier and harder to stay. It was so tempting to forget everything that drove her need for self-control.

"I didn't mean that. I'm sorry that people are ignorant." Her skin prickled, unsure of his reaction. He boomed out a laugh.

"Don't be sorry for that! You'll spend your life apologising." He chuckled as he navigated the car through the traffic, heading towards Circular Quay. A courier van pulled out in front of him, and he slammed his left hand on the horn. A vigorous curse punched the air, before he swallowed.

"Shit. I'm sorry—" He breathed deeply. "—I'm trying to have more patience."

"No road rage for you?" A giggle rose in her throat and she pinched her lips together.

He exhaled, a manly sigh of epic proportions. "It's the car. … No, it's me."

"Oh?"

"When I got this car, I loved it. The freedom of just driving. Going anywhere I wanted."

"And being a man, you were impatient when people got in your way?"

"Yeah, something like that."

"What changed?" She clenched her fists. Goddamn curiosity. If her head was in charge, she'd be able to shut her mouth and keep this just about sex.

"I flipped the bird at a guy who cut in front of me at the lights. He slammed on the brakes, leapt out and knocked on the window. I thought he was going to rip open the door and punch me."

She gasped, staring at him. "What did you do?"

"I realised that I couldn't get out and stand toe to toe with him. He would get a free shot and there'd be nothing I could do about it."

"Oh no. What happened?"

Joey loved telling this story because everyone always gasped at that bit as they imagined him stuck in the car unable to stand up and defend himself. There was a lot to process in that response—the sheer ableism for a start—and he'd come to a point where he enjoyed making people think a bit harder about their assumptions.

"Luckily, this dickhead's missus got out of his car and started screaming at him not to be a fool. He turned around to yell at her, and the lights turned green. Everyone jumped on their horns…"

"That sounds bananas."

"Yeah, a bit. Anyway, he scarpered." Joey had been irritated when she'd apologised, but once he understood that she was upset that people were idiots, the rankle disappeared.

"Wow. Thank fuck for that," she said. He risked taking his eyes off the road for a second to glance at her. She toyed with the lowest button on her jacket. She didn't have her bag today, the one she used as a barrier between her and the world.

"I don't believe in fate, but I wonder sometimes if stuff like that is there to teach you a lesson or something." He frowned at the stream of cars waiting at the lights as he slowed down.

"Maybe you were just ready to listen to the lesson?" Was she listening to the lesson he'd put in the story? He'd like to think she understood. She'd shown her understanding so far, and he knew how long it'd taken him to unlearn all his ableist assumptions when he'd first been injured. People like Ella were a gift because she was willing to learn. Ironic really given her retort just now.

"I guess so." He eased the accelerator stick towards him as the traffic light changed, following the other cars along Young St, down the hill towards Circular Quay.

"On the plus side, you didn't actually get punched to have to figure out that maybe road rage isn't a cool idea."

"Are you laughing at me?" He glanced at her again to see her smirk.

"A little."

"Okay." He flicked the indicator and made the sharp turn into the parking building.

"Don't you want to know why?" Her voice had a cheeky note in it.

"Why don't you tell me?"

"It's just so typical of a man. You can't figure out that antagonising some bogan fuckwit is a silly idea until he punches you in the face."

"He didn't actually hit me."

"Therefore you are saying you are an enlightened man?" She guffawed, almost choking on a laugh.

"I'm not making any claims about my manliness. You've seen enough to make that judgement yourself."

"Touché. Definitely all man."

He glanced at her pink cheeks, then had to swallow away the growing desire so he could concentrate on navigating the tight turning carpark. He lined up the disabled park, and reversed neatly in.

"Nice," she whispered. "I didn't know there was parking under this building."

"It's one of the benefits of this little blue sticker. There are disabled spots all over the city in places that aren't available to everyone. And this park is sweet, it's basically opposite Quay View and is only used by the staff in the building above us."

"I really like how you've embraced your situation. It doesn't seem to stop you doing anything."

"Why should it? In the unit, one of the peer support guys—a great bloke called Steve—said to me your whole life you've been defined as an athlete. It would be easy to allow your chair to define you. Try not to fall into that trap, instead figure out what else you have to offer the world."

She tilted her head, the way she always did when she was choosing her words carefully. "Did that help?"

The pause before she answered made him wonder how many questions she'd dismissed before asking that one. He wanted to gather her in his arms, to tell her to ask them all, but it was probably too soon to go there, especially when she was still a bit jumpy around him. He didn't want her to run away again.

"Yeah. I realised I would have had to have figured that

out soon even if I hadn't been injured. I was nearing retirement. My body was already showing signs that my career would be finished soon."

Ella spoke softly. "Sport can't go on forever, I suppose."

"That's the truth of it. Once I'd seen that, it was easy to plan a future because accident or not, I would've needed to have done that. There are so many cool toys that make the daily challenges easier. It's simply a matter of choosing to use them."

"You touched on that in your talk. Thanks for sharing a more personal version." She'd reverted to that formal lawyer tone, the one she used whenever their conversation got a bit close to something like a real connection. He let that one go. If he pushed her too hard, she might leave and he wasn't ready for that yet.

"How about that drink? Do you mind getting out, so I can grab my chair?" He probably shouldn't think too hard about why the idea of her leaving made his chest tighten.

"Oh. Sure." She clambered out quickly to stand tense and straight beside the car. He leaned into the back seat, tugged his folded chair over, and lifted it out of the car. The lightweight design was easy to move. Normally he just tossed it on the front passenger seat, the extra twist to get it out of the back made the whole manoeuvre take longer and put extra pressure on his body. He flicked it open, then called out.

"Hey, would you mind grabbing that sheepskin from the back seat for me?"

"Okay." She opened the door, picked up his covers, "this one?"

"Yeah, thanks."

A little smile lingered on her lips. He hoped it meant that she was pleased to be asked, even though she seemed to hover between wanting to be involved in his life and staying detached. She walked around the car to pass him the cover that would provide him some comfort in his chair. Their fingers touched, a zing chasing up his arm, as he took them from her. She cleared her throat and stepped backwards.

"Come on, let's go and you can tell me why you don't like Stu." If she wanted to stick to work, then he may as well direct the conversation to a topic that told him more about her, while also pretending to be work. He pressed the button to lock his car and rolled towards the exit.

She walked beside him, her stride length matching his speed comfortably. "What? Where did that come from?"

"Just a gut feel from watching you in that meeting."

"I like Stu. He can't help that he has every advantage."

"Take care not to sound too jealous."

She sighed, stopping, and he braked beside her. "I'm not jealous. I know I sound curt sometimes, it's just hard to make myself heard in that room full of charming marketers. They don't want to hear the lawyer naysaying their great ideas, but they need to hear it."

"I understand. It's a tough gig, but someone has to do it."

She wrinkled her nose, and the sun glinted off her earring as she turned towards him. "Being on the Exec team at Kapow is a great career opportunity. I intend to make the most of it."

7

The foyer, decorated with advertisements for the bar and various beverages, filled Ella with a wave of terror, her heart leaping at the sudden realisation of what she'd agreed to. "You go on up, I just have to make a quick phone call."

He nodded with no indication he'd noticed the way her voice wavered—thank God—and rolled into the lift without her. She swiped her phone and called her best friend who answered after a couple of rings.

"Sal."

"What's the matter, hon?" Sal replied quickly.

"I've got a dilemma."

"What is it?"

"I've been asked out for a drink this afternoon—" Ella paused. She rested against the cool brick wall.

"Say no. You are good at that." She could almost hear Sal shrug at the other end of the line, and only moments after she'd called herself a naysayer too. Sal didn't mean it like that though.

"There's the dilemma. I already said yes."

"Oh. I see. Well, you have two options."

"Yeah?"

"Yeah. Either you don't drink and tell the person why. Or you have one drink and stop stressing about it. You aren't your mother." Sal's matter-of-fact statement covered a long history of talking about this issue.

"You know that it's not that simple."

"It is. It really is." She heard the exasperation in Sal's tone. And no wonder, they'd been over and over this territory for years. Maybe Sal was right. She leaned her head back against the bricks, the weight of guilt pressing down on her chest. It'd be so simple to walk away now, to be a coward and run from Joey again, to pretend that none of this mattered.

"Who is it?" Sal gasped. "Not Joey again?"

"Yes." Ella whispered.

"Oh my God, Ella."

"I shouldn't have told you." She toyed with her earring, twisting it around.

"Yes, you should. What good is a best mate if you can't tell them all the details. Have you been holding out on me, hon? Sharing is caring!"

Ella rolled her eyes and smiled. Some of the weight lifted and she raised her head. "If it was just sex, then yeah, it'd wouldn't be a drama. But he's so…"

"Charming, rich, good looking, great in bed? I don't see

a problem." Sal laughed, that infectious laugh that always calmed Ella because she knew she wasn't alone in the world.

"Fine. I'm going to have a drink with him."

"Good for you. How did this come about anyway? I thought you weren't going to ring him till the weekend?"

"It's a long story."

"I always have time for your stories."

"Hmmm, well, you know how I made the Exec team..." Ella stood up straight as Sal screamed down the phone, a full on squeal of excitement.

"Holy shit, girlfriend. That's amazing."

"Yeah. Yeah, it is. You screamed like that last time I told you too!" Ella sighed as warm satisfaction spread through her body, easing the tension in her neck and shoulders.

"But how does that get you to drinks in the afternoon with Joey? Shouldn't you be at work?" Sal paused, then gasped. "Oh. My. God. Joey is on the Exec team too? Shit, hon, you are fucked now."

Giggles bubbled out, almost hysterical as all the tension of the morning released. Ella slid down the wall, resting on her heels, as she gulped through the laughter. "No," she said eventually on a shaky breath. "He's not on the team, but a new project was announced today, and I have to do all the contracts to put it in place, including the one between him and Kapow. It's complicated." Or maybe it wasn't.

"So you have to work with him, and that freaks you out, because?"

"Because I've just made the Exec and I need to look professional."

"Hence why you are hiding somewhere talking to me,

instead of having a quiet drink to discuss 'work' with him." Damn Sal and her insights. 'Work' indeed.

"Yeah."

"Take a big breath. Fix your mascara. Go and have that drink. One glass of wine won't turn you into your mother."

"Yes, boss."

"You know it, darl." Sal laughed. Ella waited till Sal hung up. Thank fuck for friends. She pushed against the wall to stand up and pressed the up button on the lift. A few minutes later, she slid into the seat opposite Joey and put her notepad and pen on the floor next to her chair.

"Sorry about that." What had possessed her to carry that inside, rather than leave it in his car? The pretence of doing work, that's what. "That took much longer than I anticipated."

"It's fine. What do you want?"

"Control and power." Shit. She clapped her hand over her mouth and her heart thundered in her chest. She hadn't meant to blurt that out. He looked quizzically at her, and no wonder. What kind of person said that? What was it about him that inspired brutal honesty?

"I meant what do you want to drink?"

"Oh, right. That's an excellent question." Ella stalled, Sal's voice arguing in her head with her own habit. Was it just a habit? Or was it crucial to maintain her controls? Sitting opposite Joey, who waved the drinks menu at her, made it impossible to decide.

"What will you have?" she asked. "I'll go to the bar and grab them."

"It's fine. I've been here before. They do table service for me."

"The perks of being famous?" She smiled. Yeah, reminding him of that fact wasn't going to make this any less bloody awkward. She wanted to sink through the floor and disappear.

"Yeah, that'd be it. I'm having a beer if that makes any difference to your decision." He raised one eyebrow, a quirk that made his rich brown eyes shine with unreleased laughter. Goddamn it, how did he put her off-balance like this all the time? If it was simply sex, it'd be easy, but every moment she spent with him added complexity to the way she viewed him. She liked him. It shouldn't be a problem, yet it was. A fucking massive problem. She couldn't just find bodily pleasure with him, then walk away. If she didn't like him, she wouldn't even be here.

"Decisions, decisions. It'll be easier if you give me that menu you are waving about the place," she said. He tossed the menu on the table between them, and she grabbed it.

"Don't hide behind it, you've done enough hiding from me today."

She lowered the menu and peered at him. "I don't know what you mean."

He snorted. "Yes, you do. You've created a wall to keep me away."

"Most of today we've been in a meeting. I've been working. I'm not sure what you expect?" She suspected, with a sinking feeling in her stomach, that he saw more than she wanted him to see.

"Why do you want to keep me at a distance? We've

already been pretty close." He leaned forward, his elbows on the table, with a hungry expression on his face. Ella fought the urge to shrink away. She lifted her chin and tried to let herself enjoy the power in the moment. He wanted her and it made her veins sing with anticipated desire.

"Physically close." If only she could keep their interaction so simple, but her mouth ran off by itself again. "And yeah, I'd like to experience that again." She swallowed. It broke every one of her rules.

"I would like that too." His eyes darkened to an impossible black pool of desire. He reached out and stroked one finger down her jawline, sending a skitter of sparks across her skin. She sucked in a sharp breath, inhaling his masculine scent layered with a smidgen of sweet amber and notes of spice and eased the breath out as a long sigh when he dragged his rough fingers over the soft skin of her chin. When he brushed his thumb over her bottom lip, she closed her eyes and let herself drift into the heat blossoming down to her core.

"What is it about you that makes me want to—" She stopped short of saying it aloud.

"Same." His deep voice rumbled between them. Her eyes flickered open. It took only a tiny movement to close the gap between them and press her lips against his. He tasted like home, an idea that scared the pants off her, but also made her want to rip off her pants and stay with him forever. Would she, could she, indulge herself with him? She'd never let anyone this close before. She didn't even want him close, he just seemed to end up there, naturally.

"Stop thinking." He broke their kiss and she immediately felt the lack of him.

"Hey love birds, what will you have?" The waiter interrupted her thoughts, it should have been a welcome relief, but instead her body scowled at the waiter, wanting him to disappear so she could press herself against Joey. She shook her head at the chaos banging inside her brain.

"Just an orange juice for me." She needed some semblance of normal in her life, a little control over her destiny.

"I'll have a beer. This one." Joey pointed at the menu, and the waiter nodded.

"No problem, sir. I'll be back in a moment." He left, leaving only awkwardness between them. Ella glanced up at Joey and grimaced at the way his mouth quirked up at one side.

"How can you be okay with this?" She didn't even know what she was asking. Okay with what exactly? Being here together?

"How can you not? Look at that view, the sun glinting off the water, the sharp white tiles of the Opera House. This is the life." The quirk in his lip spread into a proper smile. One that curled her toes at the charm aimed her way.

"Never mind. Let's get this contract nailed down. We have a standard one. Do you want me to run through the conditions?" She deliberately changed the subject back to work.

"I have to be honest, Wiremu, he's my agent, does all the bookings for my speaking, and so on. He did the deal with

Kapow and he is the one to talk to about the contract details."

"Aren't you the least bit interested in what you are signing up for?"

"I trust him."

"So this whole…" She waved her hand. "…thing has nothing to do with work?" She didn't like being tricked. "If you are genuine, you'll at least do some work right now."

"Here you are, sir. One beer, and an OJ."

"Thanks." Joey lifted his beer to his mouth. Ella's eyes tracked the liquid as it flowed against his lips. She wanted to know how the cool fluid would taste on his warm lips. She sipped her juice, a nice tart citrus tang with the texture of freshly squeezed juice, little bursts on her tongue. His damned body distracted her—again—from her task.

"Fair enough. Let's go over all the terms and conditions and whatnot that gets lawyers all excited. But first, can I ask a question?" he said. She nodded slowly, even though her stomach twisted at the idea.

"There were some pretty big tensions between you and Stu in that meeting. What do I need to know?"

"You are misinterpreting it. Stu is good. He's on my side, I think."

"You think?"

"I've only recently been made part of the Executive team at Kapow, and pretty much only because the previous in-house legal consul left to run his own firm. I've already mentioned that I come across as a negative Nancy, and I'm still learning how to navigate the politics of the Exec team.

Plus, if you haven't noticed, I don't quite fit, and I need to prove that I am up to the job."

"Don't undersell yourself. They still had to choose you; they could have gone external."

"Thanks. It is a huge opportunity." It really was. Sal would tell her to celebrate it, not going hunting for all the nasty loopholes. Undoing years of training on that aspect wasn't going to happen anytime soon though. "Today I was annoyed at Stu for the surprise. I'm supposed to sign off on all the deals before they get announced. That's all you were seeing."

"Makes sense. So how are you going to do prove yourself, then?"

She blew out a long breath, but it did nothing to ease the flutter in her stomach. "The only way I know. Hard work and sheer bloody minded-ness? Through actions; that's how our family have always succeeded." She thought back to Baba's real estate business, and the long hours he'd put in to make it a success, and to her great-great-grandfather who'd started it all. "My great-great-grandfather's name was Quong Tart, and it's because of him that I have this memorable surname. He was a Chinese immigrant who came from poverty to own an entire floor of QVB."

"Bloody hell, that's impressive."

She nodded, ready to spill more of her family's story.

"It doesn't translate well, does it?" He asked, and thankfully without the snide smirk she expected from people when discussing her name.

"No—" Ella grinned ruefully, "—but it's our heritage

and I want to honour the name. There's even a statue of him in Ashfield."

"Holy fuck. He must have done some impressive things, then. None of my relatives have statues," he said. She wanted to drink in the admiration in his voice and took a sip of her juice instead. He waited with his hands spread, as if to say, tell me everything. God, she was tempted, just to unburden herself to him. It was too soon and he would think it meant too much, so she gave her head a quick shake and swallowed. Focus on great-times-whatever-grandpa.

"Yeah, he came here as a kid from China, and worked on the gold fields in Victoria. He made a fortune there, then came to Sydney and made another selling imported goods from his homeland, silks and tea, mostly. He basically founded Ashfield, that's why the statue of him is there." It was much easier talking about him than about her own dramas.

He chuckled. "Can you imagine what Stu would say if you mentioned this?"

"Fuck no, don't go there." She sat back in her chair and folded her arms. "Now that is a man I'd love to meet. A real man of drive, with a well developed instinct for success, that much is obvious. I'm sure we could do marvellous things for him." Her mimicking of Stu wasn't even that good, at least not her version of Stu's voice. Joey's laughter warmed her. The words were pretty accurate, and a wave of joy filled her torso as she made Joey laugh. The only problem was that her mockery came at a cost. She sounded like an asshole.

"I'm sorry. I shouldn't mock Stu. I like him. He's been kind to me when he didn't necessarily need to be." She sighed. "Plus I've only just started this job, it's too early to be marked as troublesome." Once more he'd dragged the truth out of her before she realised it.

"Because you won't be accepted as part of the team." His eyes widened and his mouth softened. He appeared to truly understand the core of her problem with his presence at the meeting today.

"Yeah." Her shoulders slumped, and she stared at her orange juice, tracing the condensation on the outside of the glass.

"You wouldn't be on the team if you hadn't earned it."

8

"True." Ella sat up straight and stared at him unblinking. Joey could see her brain churning behind those rich brown eyes. She tapped her fingers on her bottom teeth, then grabbed her pen, scribbling a circle on the notepad she'd left on the table.

"Gimme a sec." A lock of her black hair had escaped the tight bun she had pulled it back into, and it stroked the edge of her cheek as she madly scribbled notes. The focus and intensity made his mouth water, while his fingers hovered, wanting to feel the silk of her hair caress over his fingertips.

"Do you know how hot that is?" He let his ragged breathing infuse his whisper so she would know how much he was affected.

Her head flicked up. "What?"

"The energy you have poured onto the page. It's hot." Heat prickled his cheeks as she stared at him with rampant curiosity.

"Really?"

"Yeah…" He blinked as the air crackled with electricity between them, like the way a storm rolled over the ocean towards his cliff-top house. She placed her pen on the table, a deliberate, exact motion, and she stared at him with her head slightly ajar and her soft lips parted.

"Hold that thought." She dropped her gaze to the page.

"How long should I hold it for?" he asked. She lifted her face to his, a small smile on her face, with her rich brown eyes dancing.

"Until we get to your house." She gulped her orange juice, her tongue flicking out to lick a drip from the edge of her lip. It was his turn to stare unblinking at her. Had she just propositioned him?

"My house?" His voice came out with a rasp, and he cleared his throat.

"Yes. I'm too old for sex in the toilets of a bar." She rolled her eyes, then grinned. "Won't your house be more comfortable? Private?"

He smiled. She did want what he wanted.

"And I can take my time with you," he said. She shivered, and her face glowed. For a long moment, they stared at each other, until she broke the spell to stand up, grabbing her notepad.

"Excellent. I hope you don't mind, but I'm going to work while you drive. I want to finish these notes, send a few emails." She shrugged lightly and he wished she would stop apologising for being competent.

Instead, he nodded. "Sure. It's an efficient use of time."

"Yes! Exactly." Her enthusiasm infused her whole body, and he wanted to say more pithy statements that she agreed with. He tucked a fifty dollar note under his hardly touched beer and rolled backwards. It was way too much for two drinks but he didn't care. Every fibre of his body was focused on Ella, and he wasn't about to let a minor thing like paying for drinks distract him.

"Shall we?" He gestured towards the lift, then followed her as she walked with purpose before him. She wore a different elegant suit to the night they'd met, and this one also highlighted her curves, from her neat hair down her straight back, all the way down past her round bottom, slim legs and skinny high heels.

Half an hour's drive later, he pressed the button to open his garage door, and glanced across at Ella. True to her word, she had scribbled notes, and typed frantically into her phone for the entire half hour drive to his house. He'd put on an old Hilltop Hoods album, tapping out the rhythm on his steering wheel with his left thumb. She didn't seem to notice as she worked. Traffic had been fairly easy by Sydney standards, too early for the main rush hour, and he'd navigated the streets to Coogee automatically. Anticipation had built in his torso, a warmth that spread over his chest and shoulders, growing as the simple act of sharing his car, sharing the same air as her, became almost intimidating. A tremor ran over the back of his neck, surely he wasn't nervous? Damn it, he was. He scratched his head, then eased the car down the ramp into the basement garage of his house, trying not to clench the steering wheel. He parked the car and turned off the engine.

"We are here." Clever words evaded him.

"Oh." She raised one finger in the air. "Hang on a second. I'll just finish this." Her thumbs flew on her phone, as all her attention soaked into the small device. The tension in his shoulders eased as he watched her focus. He'd been right back at Quay View, seeing her work was hot. The energy she exuded was incredible; a reminder of the way she'd focused on him the other night. He swallowed away the remnants of nerves that had grown as he drove, and simply waited as she poured herself into her task.

She hit 'send' with a flourish and turned to him with a little grin. "There, all done." He reached for her, gliding his finger over her cheek, and she leaned in. He breathed in, soaking up her proximity, the vanilla scent of her skin rinsing over him. Never again would he associate vanilla with boring, forever more, it would be the smell of her energy, her drive, simply her.

"Joey." She whispered his name reverently as she closed the gap between him. She brushed her lips against his, a promise of more, the drizzle on a hot summer day that sizzled the pavement as a thunderstorm hung heavy in the air. The promise of a torrent to break a drought. He took that promise, sliding his hands into her hair and pressing his lips against hers. Firm. Needing to take everything she offered. Her eyes opened wider, darkening as she opened her mouth. Had she succumbed to his pressure, or had he to hers? Maybe their need mixed together to create this blend of strength, of power that surged in his veins and roared in his ears. Her hands grasped his biceps, her fingers digging deep as his tongue sank into her mouth, tasting her essence. Bursts of her flavour surrounded him.

"Holy fuck." He murmured and she laughed into his mouth.

"Indeed." She managed to make that one word full of precision and pleasure, a nod to how much he enjoyed seeing her wrangle the legal world to fit her goals, and it was all he could do to not dive into her. His fingers tightened on her skull. She sighed against his mouth, almost a moan. She must moan. It became a driving need inside him to draw a moan of pleasure from her lips, as he spread his hand wider over her head, while kissing her hard. Her hair succumbed to his desire, falling out of the pins over the backs of his hands, silky, soft, like the fabric she'd swept over his lap on their first night. She shifted closer, her breasts pressing against his chest. Thunk. A quiet thud interrupted.

"Oh, shit, my phone." She pulled back with an annoyed frown.

"Forget it." He didn't want to move, but he let her go, his hands drifting down to her shoulders.

"Yeah, you're right."

Yes, I am right. Forget your phone, focus on me. He opened his mouth to tell her, but only an odd sound came out, something between a groan and the beginnings of a command.

"Joey." The frown disappeared and she wrinkled her nose. "Maybe we should go inside?"

He wretched himself away. It made sense to go somewhere more comfortable, even as his body screamed at him to stay. Her hair trailed over his skin, as he eased his hands away, down her arms. The fabric of her jacket rough under his fingertips, not actually rough, only rougher than her smooth skin. He grasped her hands, threading his fingers between hers, needing to maintain the connection as his pulse galloped. They waited, just breathing each other's air, holding hands. He wanted to catalogue this moment. She was the first to move, pulling her hands away, leaving his cool as she opened the car door, letting in the sullen, humid air of his garage.

"How do you set this up?" she asked. He shook his head to gather himself back into the real world. She stood outside his driver's side door, with his folded chair in her hands. He'd been so lost in the moment that he hadn't noticed her move around the car. He wanted to throw away the niggling doubt about why she spent time with him, that his fame meant more than he did. If he was honest with himself, and he typically was, he wanted her in his life. Enough to ignore reason. She tapped on the window. He opened the door and seeing her there with his chair made him abandon reason.

"Stop thinking. It's only sex," she said. A voice clambered in his head, taunting him with a whisper, 'this could be more.' He pulled in a deep breath, one that filled his lungs all the way to the bottom, and let the oxygen burst through his body.

"See that clip?" He pointed to his chair, "yeah, that one. Unclip that, watch your fingers, and the chair unfolds."

"Clever. So simple, and effective." She unfolded the chair and set it on the ground for him. He reached out, and secured it, before grabbing his cushions and covers. The set up and transfer came easily after all the practice he'd had, an automatic set of movements that was part of his life now. Ella stepped back. How did she know that he required a bit more space? She had a natural way about her that allowed him to relax and concentrate on her; on the broader questions of whether she would fit emotionally in his life. He shook his head, and slammed the door shut beside him. His instincts screamed that she would fit perfectly in his life, into an Ella shaped hole that he hadn't realised existed.

"The lift to the rest of the house is over there." He pointed in the direction and hoped she wouldn't notice the tremble in his hand.

"Behind the boat? Is this whole garage yours?" Her eyes darted around the space.

"You make it sound obscenely massive. It's only a three car garage, not that big." He'd seen bigger ones in this suburb.

"Three! Is that including the boat? God, where I grew up, a ten-metre frontage was a double sized block." She shifted her bag on her shoulder.

"Ashfield, right?"

"Yeah." She huffed out an annoyed laugh. "Only a few weeks ago, I was walking from the train station, when some lout called out 'go home.' And I stared at him, thinking 'what? It's just over there.' It took a few minutes for me to realise that he meant to China. What the fuck, dude, I've never even been to China!" She pressed her fingers against her nose and made a snuffled noise.

"Don't cry. He's not worth your tears," he said. She dropped her hand, a huge grin spread across her face.

"I'm not sad. It's hilarious. People are so fucking frustrating, but what can you do but laugh. I mean, seriously, some kid comes to Ashfield, a suburb founded by my Chinese ancestor, and wants me to go home. You go the fuck home to wherever the bland hell you come from." Her voice rose in strength, his admiration rising too. He understood why she didn't judge him on the one issue that others defined him by, his chair. No wonder he could visualise life with her. He blew out a sharp breath. He stretched out, and grabbed her hand, stroking his thumb over her palm. Maybe he did it only to reassure himself, but she smiled at him, soft and warm.

"Where did you say that lift was again?"

"Behind the boat." He started to let her hand go. She curled her fingers over his to maintain the contact between them. The thud of his heart echoed in his ears, as an aroused tingle spread up his arm, and across his shoulders. She started to walk, and he let her pull him along, his other hand on one wheel to help steer. She pushed the button, and the lift doors opened, the glass wall at the back showing only the stone wall of the lift shaft. Together, they glided inside, and he pushed the button for the top floor.

"Watch." He pointed to the glass. He loved this house, the way the lift rose up out of the basement, soaring into the sky with the glorious view over the ocean and its varying moods. She turned to look out, just as natural light poured in from the sea, filtered through the grand glass walls, across his lounge and into the lift. Her hand stayed in his, trailing behind her as she gasped at the view. Her shoulders rose, then fell slowly as she let the breath out. Yeah, the view always made his lungs fill and contract like that too. They arrived at the top floor, the view narrowing to a hallway that allowed the view to be maintained for the whole journey. The doors behind slid open, and he rolled back, tugging at her hand. She pulled her hand free and spun around to face him.

"I … How spectacular. I could ride that lift all day." Ella's breathless whoosh of words filled the volume of the elevator.

"It's pretty neat." He loved this house, how it worked for him, and connected him to nature as he entered it. And the extra expense to get all this glass was worth the cost because the view was worth more than money.

"Neat? It's amazing."

"Wait till you see my room." His teasing had the right effect as her cheeks flushed pink, and those delightful soft lips opened a fraction.

"Show me." She followed him, as he rolled backwards into the house. Down one side of the lift shaft were a few guest rooms, with a small living room that they shared, and on the other was his personal space. A massive bedroom with private balcony that overlooked the ocean, and an equally massive bathroom, set up to make access easy for him. The viewing hallway was part of the guest side of the house, wrapping around the lift shaft, while his side had a double width entry door near the lift doors. He only shut that door when he had guests over, which was pretty often given the size of his whanau. He spun his wheels, still going backwards, his eyes tracking Ella as she followed him, her eyes flicking around his house.

She shook her head. "This place—" A smug warmth

settled over him as she stared in awe at her surroundings. "—you need some decent art, though. I mean, on that side of the lift, you have the ocean, so those walls need no adornment, but over here, you could do with some colour."

"Do you think so?"

"I wouldn't have said it if I didn't think so. A friend of mine runs a little gallery in Summer Hill, she'd know just the right thing to put here. Something bright and cheery, to pull the outdoor light down the corridor into this hall."

"Stop talking, Ella."

9

He'd noticed that she babbled a little when nervous, and he couldn't help but be pleased that she felt … something too. He squeezed her hand, to reassure her, but of course, she bounced towards him, surprising him with boldness. She slid onto his lap, wrapped her hands around his neck, and licked his ear. Bolts of lust sent any doubt into rapid retreat as her body pressed, insistent, against his.

"You promised me an impressive bed," she whispered, her lips soft against his ear. He stroked his hand up her back, opening his mouth to answer, when she nipped at his ear lobe. Heat shot down his neck, across his shoulders. Heat that would have zipped down his spine before, but now spread through his changed nervous system, raising the hairs on his arms in anticipation.

"I did." He dropped his hands off her back and grabbed his wheels. He spun them around, so quickly that her loose hair flicked over her shoulders, caressing his face. A promise. She squealed and grabbed him tighter.

He grinned. "You are safe with me."

"Because you are a good driver?" She buried her face against his neck, her voice muffled.

He chuckled. "Yeah." One skim of his wheels, and they sped along the wooden floors, designed to make it easy for him to speed around the house without much effort on his shoulders. Another sent them past the door to his giant bathroom, then the short hallway opened up to reveal the ocean, fully on display through a huge glass wall. He had no neighbours between him and the sea, and he loved it. Every single time he rolled in here, he smiled.

"Look up." He commanded and he watched carefully as Ella lifted her head and turned to the view.

"Oh. Oh. Oh, wow. That is … well, I'm sure if I was a writer, I could find something better to say than wow. But wow—" Her breathy response was everything he hoped for, that she would love his house the same way he did.

"Yeah, I like it."

"Like it? I fucking love it. You lucky bastard, living here." She glanced around the room, her gaze settling on his bed, "and fucking waking up to this every day. Holy balls." She grabbed his face, and kissed him full on the lips, no holding back. His instinct was to wrestle for power, to soak up her enthusiasm. Instead, he waited, toying with her, gently sliding his hands up her arms, to rest on her shoulders as she devoured him. Desire rushed in his veins, heat and Ella, flooding his senses. Her fingers gripped his temple, and he pulled back just enough to talk.

"I want you on my bed." He panted, breathless with urgency. She lifted her head, nodding, and let her hands drift down his throat. Her fingertips trailed heat, burning with promise, as she pressed her palms against his chest. His heart thumped so hard, she must be able to feel it beating. A little sly grin flickered at the edge of her mouth, and her eyes were dark with desire, almost black pools of longing that made his lungs fill with breath until his chest puffed out into her hands. The grin grew as she slipped off his lap. She sat, almost primly, on the edge of his bed, and bent over to unbuckle her shoes. The neatness of her created a juxtaposition against the frantic kiss they'd shared. He had no clue how to describe the shoes, except that his gaze locked onto her fingers as they grazed her ankles.

"Are you coming?" she asked. *Yes. Far too soon.* He transferred from his chair to the bed, shuffling a few pillows around him out of habit. She flung her shoes off, and rolled towards him, her hands scrambling up his legs.

"You know I can't feel that," he said with a slight shrug.

"Yeah, but I want all of you." She clambered onto her knees and tugged frantically at his shirt to release it from his pants. Pure enjoyment soared through his body, at her simple and complete acceptance of him.

"Keep going." His voice came out rusty, and she purred, the sound vibrating out of her. He grabbed her jacket, flicking open the buttons, and soon clothing flew everywhere. He glimpsed navy blue lace as she flung off her bra, her back arching so her breasts dominated his view. Her hands were everywhere on him at once, as she sat across his lap, her knees either side of his bare legs and aching, hard cock. He wrapped his hands around her, to drag her down onto him, and their skin connected in a sizzle.

"Ella." Her name spilled out with reverence as he kissed her, his mouth finding hers in a rush. She moaned, sliding her body against his, so her tight nipples dragged against his chest.

"Condom?" she asked as his heart thumped against hers. His busted nervous system sent fireworks shooting along his shoulders and arms, the ones that used to hum in his torso, now spilled broader. Her fingers traced his biceps, traced the edges of fire, and his head tipped back against the bed's headboard. She bit his upper lip, and a shock of power surged in him. He rolled them both, so he lay onto top of her, cradling her face in his hands.

"Do you want this?" He had to slow them down before he burst.

"Oh my god, yes. You've barely touched me, and I'm so ready." Her words sent a fresh surge in him, his cock twitched against her legs, only wanting her more, all thoughts of slowing vanished. He reached out with one hand for the drawer at his bedside and pulled out a condom. She snatched it from him, the foil cool between their hands for a second before she pushed him on the chest. He shifted so he lay beside her, kissing the tender skin on her neck. She shivered as he moved his hands across her throat, her pulse beating rapidly under his thumb, and down to cup her breasts. Her nipples pebbled as he brushed his thumbs over her, her moan and a waft of vanilla filling the air.

"Now. Please." She echoed his thoughts. He smiled against her neck, kissed her shoulder, as he let one hand drift lower, spreading over her stomach. He lifted himself on one elbow, removing his left hand and replacing it with his mouth on her breast. She took advantage of his new position, fumbled with the foil, ripped it open, and rolled the condom down his length. Her fingers on his shaft sent a shiver up his back, made his chest muscles tremble. He sucked the tight bud of her nipple, and she let out a sob, the sound of promise in her capitulation. She wasn't leading this charge anymore; he'd taken control, and he revelled in it. Her hands, so previously frantic dropped onto his hips, right on the boundary of his ability to feel. No matter, because his hands could feel, his mouth could feel, and he used all of that to glide his fingertips down through her curls. He played with her, moving over her clit to draw out her voice, little sighs that nearly undid him, as her pleasure built. He flicked his tongue over her nipple, and she arched.

"Now, Joey, damn you." Her breath whispered against his skin. His cock responded, hardening more than he thought possible, pressing against her hip. She grabbed his hand, pressing his palm against her wet slit with an urgency that thrilled him. He slipped two fingers inside, giving her no warning, as he sunk his fingers into her heat.

"Yes. Yes. More." She pleaded and sobbed for him, her hips lifting to press against his hand. He thrust once more with his fingers, with the base of his palm against her clit, and she came undone, slickness tightening around his fingers. As the last tremor raced over her body, and she started to go limp beside him, he rolled them both, so she lay replete on top of him. He grabbed her arse, her petite, round arse, and squeezed tight. Her head jerked up, with her lazy, sated gaze staring at him. He lifted her, and she gasped. She drew her knees up beside him, positioning her body to receive him. The head of his shaft found her entrance, and she shifted to ease him in. He held her arse tight, held her poised, as her fingertips dug into his shoulders.

"Joey. Stop playing."

"Playing is the best part. It's better for both of us to take our time," he rasped. His biceps trembled.

"Next time, you can play. I need you now." He released his hold, slid his hands up to her lower back, as she rocked her hips, filling herself on his cock, surrounding him with liquid heat that tightened around him. He wanted to pump himself into her, frustration at his injury driving into his hands as he grasped her hips to move her where his hips couldn't. *Help me.* She undulated her spine, drawing herself up onto her knees. She stared at him with her lips parted, the expectation on her face cutting deep inside. A weird sight when the pressure of being inside her built in his balls.

"Probably not the greatest time to tell you, but I have no motion in my hips." He tried to make a joke of it, to ease the awkwardness. Her eyes flashed and he shut his eyes. Shit, he'd ruined it. But then her soft lips brushed over the indented frown on his brow.

"You silly man. Why didn't you say something earlier?" She kissed his forehead, and gently rocked back and forth, using her body to pump his cock. "I suppose you didn't want to sound unmanly."

He coughed out a laugh. "Something like that. It's not an easy comment to make."

"I didn't mind the bruises on my hips from last time, but it might have been better if you'd told me."

"Oh, by the way, I can't fuck you properly, you'll have to

do all the work." He couldn't hold back the sarcasm, and fully expected her to leave.

Instead, she glanced down to where they were joined. "Looks like you are doing a fine job fucking me now." Desire roared, searing him, as his every nerve focused on that visual. His cock rammed inside her, as she knelt above him. His hands moved on her skin, greedy for more, cupping her breasts as she moved her thighs, sliding herself up and down his cock in the perfect rhythm. Once again, killing him with her instincts for his pleasure. He slipped one hand down, running his fingertips along her folds, slick and wet, soft as they spread around his cock. She screamed his name as he rubbed her clit, her head falling backwards as she rose and fell around him. Her orgasm shuddered, sending a final thrill through his body before he lost control and came deep inside. He grabbed her hips, slamming her down onto him, as his cock throbbed with pleasure inside her. Eventually, she slumped onto him, both of them sated and relaxed. He rested his hands loosely on her back, the long strands of her hair drifting over him.

"Let me clean you up." Ella stirred as she murmured. She rolled off him, leaving him bare and cool without her body on his. She slid the condom off and rushed off to the bathroom. She better not leave again, but he didn't know what to say to keep her here. The door banged, and her head poked out.

"I've never been in a hotel this flash. Holy shit, Joey. Your house is something else."

"Ahh, never mind that. Come here to me."

"In a moment." She disappeared and after a few long

minutes, he heard the bin lid click and the toilet flush. She sauntered back into the room and flopped onto the bed on her stomach next to him.

She held her head in her hands, resting on her elbows, her expression serious. "Next time just tell me, okay."

10

"What, about the house? You could have guessed, given my profile." The frown across his brow disappeared, only to be replaced by bravado. Did she know him so well already? In such a short time, she could tell when his jokes were designed to hide. A façade to guard him from hurt. Did he think that she was here just for his wealth? Surely not?

"No." She grinned. "If I'd given that any thought, of course, I'd have figured you'd have a lovely place. No… I meant about your hips. Next time just say something. We can work it out."

"I didn't want to scare you off."

She rubbed her face. Oh, she hadn't thought about it from that point of view. "That happens? I'm sorry people are such fools. Sex isn't just about penetration."

His fake smile changed, little creases at the edge of his eyes deepening as he smiled properly. "That's what I've been told."

"Told?" She wriggled closer to him and chuckled quietly against his arm. "Surely you know you have some serious skill? Why the hesitance?"

"It's not that easy to talk about, let alone with someone I've only just met."

"Right. And since I accepted your invitation and turned up, you didn't want to send me running again?" She smiled at him, even though her stomach churned with guilt. She had run off.

"Something like that." His voice flattened. Shit. How could she explain herself?

"Look, I'm sorry about the other night. It was—" Impossible to stay. Impossible to take the risk that it might mean more than one night of pleasure.

"If it's so hard to talk about, let's not. I can think of better things to do." His offer would be so easy to grab onto.

"Better things – like sex? Say it. It's not difficult." She teased him, trailing her fingers over his tattoo, glad for the diversion away from herself. Glad to talk about sex, and not her cluster fuck of emotions.

"Sex. There you go." His mouth spread wide with a grin that teased her. Taunting her with the knowledge that he had no difficulties discussing sex. Did he know that she wanted to stay on this topic and not discuss anything deeper?

"That wasn't so hard. Given the challenges you've faced in your life—" She hesitated, unsure that she should continue. Hadn't she just blown out a breath of relief that they had steered away from emotional topics?

"Yeah, when you've had someone else wipe your arse,

and you've had to learn again how to shit for yourself, it's pretty easy to talk about sex."

"Wipe your arse?" She half sat up, blinking, and scratched the back of her neck.

He winked with his mouth curled in a half grin. "Not what you expected me to say?" She shook her head.

"No. I assumed you'd deflect somehow." She relaxed back against him, unable to resist brushing her finger along his lower lip.

"Nah, I'm the hard hitter, who takes the ball direct at the line. No side-stepping for me." And that was why she shifted the topic away from herself, but once they started, she'd have to risk everything. It was still early days between them and she wasn't sure if she wanted to open her heart and her hurts with him. Great sex would have to be enough for now.

"It's quite refreshing, especially after spending the day with lawyers and marketers who attempt to elude each other by talking in circles." She licked the end of his tattoo, tasting the remnants of salt from their earlier exertions. She rolled onto her side, to free up her hands to explore him. Over his chest muscles, down his abs, he must have such a strong core to move himself around with such ease, and it showed in the definition of each muscle. She let her fingers meander, explore, all the way down to the thin line of black hair that traced from his belly button, down to his gorgeous cock.

"What we were talking about?" His voice filled with gravel and desire, and the sound rumbled through her.

"Sex. But I know something better than talking about it," she said. She wrapped her hand around his length, sliding up to the broad head.

"Is everything a rush with you?" He had that charming twinkle in his eye, so she brushed her thumb over the head of his cock. He sucked in a sharp breath, one that made her sigh with satisfaction, sending warmth rinsing over her skin, alighting her with awareness of his proximity. Even in repose, stretched out on his massive bed beside her, he exuded supreme confidence.

"My father used to say 'shi guang liu shi, bu ke fu de'. Basically, it means time lost cannot be found again."

"Taking time to enjoy pleasure isn't time lost, it's just a different use of time." He brushed his hands along her waist, cradling the sides of her breasts, a quiet, languid movement. Gooseflesh raised on her arms as her nipples pebbled in anticipation.

"You think I should relax into this moment, not rush headlong into the next task?" She slid her hands back up his torso, over the ripples of his abdomen, and shifted so she lay half across his impressive chest.

"Yes. What if you are so busy thinking about what else you need to achieve, that you miss this moment?"

"What if I miss other opportunities because I spent time on the wrong things?"

"Time spent having fun isn't lost. Why not include more fun in your life?"

"I have fun. I schedule it." She knew she sounded defensive, as she tried to not flinch. Today, this moment right now, was unscheduled, and it worried at her, like a kitten worries the edge of a chair with its claws. She wasn't going to change her goals, and the controlled way she liked her life, to throw it away, for some bloke. Even for Joey, who called to her in a deeper way than she was ready to accept. Was it the way he accepted his situation, and turned it from disaster into success? Or was it simply the way they connected, body and brain? How every, well almost every, moment between them was easy, even as they navigated difficult topics? The only awkwardness came from her, the only reminder to herself that this wasn't the direction she'd chosen in life. A distraction, that's all he was, a temporary thrill that infused her fingertips, her lips, as her body yearned for him.

"Maybe you need to be more spontaneous, rather than attempt to schedule everything." His luscious brown eyes twinkled with humour. The combination of his chocolate eyes, and with his salty, whisky taste on her tongue, he tempted like a cocktail of delight. Only. Temporary. Desire. Her stomach churned with a blend of nerves and the ever-present heat that his proximity inspired in her. She raised her voice in an effort to keep him neatly in a compartment in her mind.

"Maybe you need to shut it about how I choose to live my—" She paused.

"No, it's not my business how you live your life." Was it just hope that she heard the unsaid 'but I want it to be'?

"What aren't you saying?"

"Ella, stop seeing judgement where there is none. You are a success."

"Thank you. That means a lot coming from you."

"What does that mean?"

"Just that I admire your brain, and especially your mental toughness." Her stomach clenched as her thoughts raced back over their conversation. She ran her hand through her hair, twisting the ends.

"You admired my resilience? On the field?" His voice had that flat tone again.

"Of course. All of Sydney admired you, even those who played against you."

He shut his eyes, shook his head once, and huffed out a breath. "That's not true. It's nice of you to say. Not true."

"Fine. I concede that one. I do read the papers. Some of that stuff is vicious. No wonder you had the mental fortitude to—"

"One challenge is much like another. There is the choice to train harder and improve, or to blame others. I saw heaps of guys give up because the training is too hard, or too early, or too often. It's the ones who work hard and try their guts out that get through."

"Your record speaks for itself." All of a sudden she realised how similar they were in their drive for success, and how talking about his achievements wasn't too far from discussing what she wanted in life. His sports career, his speaking career, and the way he approached it all, was the same as her need to succeed at work. Hard work mixed with talent, and dash of good fortune. Why did she torture herself with these conversations with him? She kept pushing him for more because she wanted to know everything about him, and yet she wasn't willing to talk about herself. No wonder his voice held a cynical note.

"I was fortunate to have talent, and family who taught me that talent isn't enough. There are so many talented kids, not all will make it."

"Talent and hard work – those are ideals that I believe in too. But what about other things like luck?" Her stomach twisted but she had to push him away with an innocuous statement. She couldn't cope if this became real; her heart might want that, but her head knew better.

"Are you teasing me?" His hands roved over her shoulders, his fingers pressing gently into the tense muscles at the base of her neck. The blend of pain and pleasure soaked in. What were they talking about? Oh, that's it. Good fortune.

"Yeah, I reckon luck must play a part. The right person watching the right game in juniors. The right coach somewhere along the way." She almost added 'the right promotion' but stopped before she once again aligned their respective careers. She spread her fingers over his smooth, brown skin, loving the way the sunlight streamed through the giant glass, painting him with shadows and highlights.

"Maybe, but only because league isn't a technical game. You can't measure players on pure statistics, so there is an element of who is watching when." His passion for his sport shone in his eyes, and a shiver of heat chased up her spine.

"Who found you?"

"Weren't you listening to my speech the other day? Or were you just anticipating our evening?"

"An admitted distraction." She licked his nipple.

"That's distracting."

"Hmmm." She hummed as she flicked her tongue over his salty skin. He tasted like man, real and masculine. Addictive.

"Let me." He rolled them both, so his large, warm body covered hers as he loomed over her, imposing, impressive.

Her skin came alight, spots of pleasure darting along like birds in the sky as his stubble brushed her cheekbones. She wrapped her arms around him, spreading her hands over the muscles of his shoulders and back.

"Joey." She breathed out his name as his teeth scraped her ear, a zinging sharpness as he flicked her earring with his tongue.

"Now it's my turn to tease."

She closed her eyes, letting her head rest back at the promise in his voice. The warmth of the summer sun through the windows was nothing compared to the heat that built in her stomach as he toyed with her. His fingers grasped her hair, small tugs at first, as he kissed down her neck. She rolled her head to the side, to expose her throat to him, unable to move much further with him hot and heavy, surrounding her.

"Bite me. I trust you." She opened her eyes to watch him, as he slid down her body. His biceps bulged with every movement. Oh, so slowly. Every shift of his skin against hers sent fire spiralling through her. She tensed, waiting for the sharp pain of his teeth.

"Do you like a little pain with your pleasure?" His lips shifted as he spoke against her neck.

"You know I do." She wanted her nerves alight with him. He kissed along her collarbone, flicked his tongue out to press against the base of her throat. Her pulse raced as he shifted again, so his mouth covered her nipple, a soft warmth that built anticipation without satisfaction. She glanced down at his black hair poised over her body. One of his huge palms slid up her side, completely covering one breast. She arched her back to press against him.

"Not yet, my impatient one." He lifted his head to speak. Immediately she missed the heat of his mouth, the warm summer air feeling cool over her naked pebbled nipple. She opened her mouth to protest. Only a whimper came out as he swooped, sucking hard on that nipple, pulling it into his mouth with the ferocity she wanted. She pleaded for more, lifting her hips against his weight. He played, holding her in that desperate place between need and blissful release. She dug her fingers in deep in his lower back, the fragment of her mind that still worked understanding that she needed to hold him where he could feel her as she pleaded for satisfaction. She ran her hands up his back, over the strong muscles either side of his spine, spreading her hands over his shoulder blades.

"Can you take more?" he asked.

"Always, and everything." She panted, her lungs rising and falling rapidly. He shifted again, kissing all the way down her body, until he stopped, just short of where she wanted him. She dug her fingers into his skull as he kissed the soft skin of her inner thigh. His timing, once again, was exquisite. Just as she started to protest his languid patience, he pounced. She shrieked, and her whole body ignited as he sunk his tongue inside her. "Holy fuck."

He pressed his finger to her clit and she came, waves of pure bliss overtaking her. She closed her eyes, sated, her hands sliding off him as her muscles relaxed in the aftermath.

"Not yet." He blew cool air over her slit, a fresh shiver of pleasure, the prospect of more, another orgasm threatening. She stretched her heavy hands to his shoulders, tracing slow circles over his skin as he simply breathed on her, slow and rhythmic. Her mouth fell open to ask what he planned, he pressed a kiss to her clit, reigniting everything. The sight of his head down there worshipping her as her legs splayed either side of him, made her heart race. Her breasts rose and fell rapidly as she panted with need, framing her view of him. He shifted again.

"Rest your legs over my shoulders." His command inspired obedience. Anything. She'd do anything for him, as his fingers explored her soft, wet folds.

"Like that?" She managed to ask. His tongue and his fingers dallied, once more building pressure inside her, pushing her towards a needy helplessness that she wanted. Craved.

"Yeah." He glanced up at her, two fingers deep inside her. His gaze added to her vulnerability making her thighs tense. Did she really want to give him all this power over her? He waited, his hands moving slowly on her, and in her, quietly easing her worry.

"Ella." He whispered her name with such a devotion that she felt like a goddess. Queen of pleasure. The tension in her thighs dissipated, replaced by a tremor.

"Yes?"

"Do you trust me?"

She managed a small nod.

"Good. I want to invade all of you."

She blinked, as curiosity roared in her ears. "Yes." Her consent came out as pure need. He'd only gifted her with pleasure, whatever he asked could only be good. The corners of his eyes crinkled, as if her simple yes meant more to him than any gift she could buy. He kissed her again once again, toying with the taut bundle of nerves, building pressure, until she arched on the bed, her heels pressing into his ribs. She begged him for more, unable to find words, only desperate cries filling the room as he spread her wide with his fingers, his tongue filling her. Just when she thought she couldn't take any more, he pressed his thumb against her arse. A round heat blossomed. She sobbed, begged for more.

"Can I?"

"Yes. Yes." She panted out her consent, desperate for him. He slid his thumb inside her arse, moving gently, somehow knowing it was her first time, while his tongue filled the rest of her in a contrasting strong rhythm. Fresh waves overtook her, and she screamed as he invaded all of her. Two different fires burned inside her, one the familiar sharp intensity of an orgasm, the other a fuller, more encompassing warmth, sensation burst into the full fireworks of the best orgasm she ever experienced. He pressed a kiss to her abdomen, as complete relaxation flowed from her core to the ends of every nerve. Her legs slid off his back, a final shiver racing up her spine as he lay against her stomach with his thumb remaining in her. He'd promised an invasion, and he'd provided more than she could have imagined. Her eyes grew heavy as her heart rate finally settled, until she slipped into a deep sleep. One she wouldn't have thought possible as his thumb remained in a connection somehow more intimate than anything she'd experienced before. A mirror to the connection growing inside her heart.

11

J oey waited until she'd drifted into a sated snooze before sliding his thumb from her body. He kissed her inner thigh, before he shifted off the bed quietly, not wanting to wake her. He transferred to his chair, rolling himself to the bathroom to wash his hands. A splash of cold water over his face did nothing to calm him, the icy freshness only sharpened his already heightened state. Ah, well, there was only one way to cure this. He grabbed his cock, the image of Ella splayed on his bed, completely giving herself to him full in his mind, and wanked until he came in great spurts onto his stomach. After a moment or few, he grabbed a cloth to clean himself up, before rolling back into his bedroom.

Ella hadn't moved. She lay on his bed, with her legs wide in relaxation, soft snores humming from her lips. He smiled. That was a sight to store away forever. It wasn't until he got closer that he noticed the gooseflesh on her skin. He spun around, racing back to the bathroom to grab a blanket from the linen cupboard. He blew a short breath out the side of his mouth. Why was he rushing? She wouldn't notice if he threw a warm blanket on her in one minute or two. She might notice if he got the damned thing stuck in his wheels and tipped himself out because he didn't take half a moment to be sensible. He gathered the blanket in his arms, rolled over to her, and flung it across her, before turning to grab his shirt off the floor where it had been thrown earlier this afternoon. The sun that had streamed in his windows earlier had faded as dusk settled over the sea. Evenings like this made him wonder what it would be like to sit on the west coast, over in Perth, and watch the sun set over the ocean. He loved the sunrise each morning, never bothering to cover the windows at night so the sun would wake him naturally. Those disused blinds were drawn over the windows on rare occasions, when he was in this room on those blindingly hot summer days when the sun glowed almost white hot in the sky. Those were the days he closed the blinds to keep the room cool.

Ella's breathy snores rid the room of silence, filling it with a soft musicality. She intrigued him with the way she blew hot and cold. One moment, staunch and bold, the next indecisive and wary. He shouldn't want to know more, to understand her, but he couldn't help himself. He wanted to find out why she hovered, uncertain at times, and help her find the bravery and confidence she exhibited in sex, and at work. He tapped his finger on his chin. It was only when they talked about her that she shrank away and hid from him. She stirred, curling herself under the blanket.

His stomach growled. He took the lift down a level to

grab a snack, leaving her to snooze. The door of his fridge glided open with an easy touch. He loved this fridge. It had been bloody expensive, imported from Japan where it had been specifically designed for wheelchair users. He scanned the contents, grabbed a couple of slices of bread. He spun around, slotting them in the toaster, then swung back to the fridge to grab butter, an avocado, and some salmon. He slid the door shut and grabbed a plate while his bread toasted. His mouth watered as the smell filled the air. He needed to refuel, a fun consequence of all that sex. He flicked the toast onto his plate, spread a good dollop of butter, before adding some salmon, slicing the avocado and piling that on top. He grabbed some salt, pepper and chili flakes to season his sandwich, before taking a massive bite. The crisp toast, warm butter, rich salmon, and smooth texture of the avocado blended into magic in his mouth. A simple, yet luxurious combination finished with a burst of tart heat from the chilli flakes.

"Mmm, that smells amazing." Ella walked into the kitchen as he took a second bite. He nodded, chewing quickly so he could respond. He swallowed, licking the last crumb off the corner of his mouth. She had wrapped his blanket around her shoulders, a naked nymph draped in fabric that hung long down her back and swirled around her legs.

"Would you like one?"

"Yes, please. I'm famished."

He spun around and slid the fridge door open.

"Oh. That is cool. What a clever, simple idea to make the door slid instead of open into you."

"Yeah, I think so. And notice how it is extra wide and shallow, rather than tall and deep, so I can reach all the levels. One slice or two?" He grabbed another avocado.

"One, thanks. I can make it."

"Nah, you are in my house. I can feed you." He put a slice of bread in the toaster. She bent down and kissed him, direct on the lips. A perfunctory brush, so natural and yet possessive all at once. Another time when he couldn't work her out.

"Thank you." She tugged the blanket tighter around herself.

"Do I bother you?"

"What, no. Yes, sometimes." The honest blurt made him smile, even though knowing it and hearing her say it made his solar plexus squirm.

"I'm mostly harmless." He aimed for a joke to ease the burr in his throat at the way her gaze sidled away. The toaster popped, with a quiet click that echoed loud in the awkward pause. He grabbed the toast with the tips of his fingers, juggling it onto the plate to avoid being burnt. She still said nothing, so he concentrated on making her food. Butter, salmon, cut the avocado, scoop it out, slice it, spread it. Twist over the salt and pepper.

"Chilli?" he asked.

"Yeah, thanks. You know, I do trust you. It's a long story." She spoke slowly, carefully. He handed her the plate with finished toast. She took it, nodding her thanks.

"I'm not going anywhere." He took another bite of his toast, the rich salmon making his tastebuds sigh with happiness.

"I ahh—" She stared at him, blinking, without eating.

"Take a bite. It'll be easier once you've eaten."

"I'm not a child." A flicker of a frown was the only change to her expression.

He raised one eyebrow as she ate. "Oh, I'm fully aware of that—" A warm glow spread over his chest as her cheeks washed with a soft pink. She chewed, her jaw muscles working, and her lips closed.

"I thought you wanted to know about me. Don't distract me." Her eyes sparkled and he wished he could retain each of those rare moments when she opened her true thoughts up to him.

"You are a continual distraction. Maybe it's one of those goose what's-it-things?" He held up hands up in front him.

She rolled her eyes. "What's good for goose is good for the gander?"

"Yeah. That's it. Now tell me why I bother you?"

"Did I say that?" She tilted her head to the side, a sly grin on her lips. "I'm sure I—"

"Oh I see, you don't really trust me."

She turned her head away from him, her focus directed to her food. A flash of fragility appeared before she blinked it away, and he wanted to stretch his arms around her. Gather her in and let her know she was safe.

"It's not that." She mumbled. "This is a difficult subject for me."

"Obviously."

She put the toast on the plate, her hand shaking a little, and eased out a long breath that ended in a shudder. Her hand holding the blanket around her shoulders glowed white across the knuckles.

"You are safe with me. If it's too difficult, I can wait." He didn't want to wait, he wanted to know what was wrong so he could fix it. He wanted to help. He reached out his hand for her. "Come and sit on the couch with me."

She placed her slim hand, tentatively, into his broad hand. Together they shifted to the large couch overlooking the ocean. She rested her head on his shoulder. "It's such a cliché really. Apparently, I have typical childhood abandonment issues and I can't commit. In fact, Sal says I refuse to commit to keep myself safe from being abandoned again." She shut her eyes, squeezed so tight, he imagined all types of terrible things that she hid from.

"So you decided to go down the use 'em and lose 'em route?"

"It's no different to any of the men at work. Why are they allowed casual sex and no one calls them on their emotional baggage?" She twisted to face him, her eyes flashing. Ahh, there was the boldness he adored!

"Maybe when they meet someone special, they have this conversation too?"

She pulled back from him. Shit too soon to mention that.

"Bullshit. You are thinking with your dick. This is sex, not anything special." The doubt infusing her voice made him want to wrap her up tight and reassure her.

"Shall I count the ways?"

"No." For a long moment he held his breath as she sat perched on the edge of the couch, only her eyes moving as she furiously examined his face. Finally, she whispered, "Yes" and he let out his breath slowly.

"You barged into my life that evening in the lift, a whisper of a promise that maybe someone would see past my chair and want to be with me."

"You asked! How could I say no?" Ella clapped her hand over her mouth. Where was this doubt in his voice coming from? From the way he presented himself to the world, she'd figured he knew he had power. Gravitas. His fame clung to him with a confidence that could only come from winning, from beating the odds of his injury, and creating a new life for himself. No wonder this situation that grew between them scared her. If he asked, she'd probably follow him anywhere. Ella nuzzled up against him, grinning against his shoulder, deliberately ignoring the growing lump of caution in her gut. If she dropped everything to follow him, what did that mean for her life?

"I hoped." Joey's simple answer dragged her back to reality.

"I think you underestimate the power you exude."

"Maybe I used to have power, strength, speed. Not anymore."

"Power isn't about physicality. The power I'm talking about comes from inside. If anything, your chair makes you seem stronger."

He scoffed, and she doubted herself too. "What? That

makes no sense." He was right, and not right. It made sense to her, the way he held himself, the way he'd adjusted and navigated life, the way he'd found a future when many would despair. Still, it didn't precisely make sense. Could she rephrase?

"Think about it this way—" She worried her bottom lip as she struggled to find an analogy. "Oh, it's like this. The chair is like a scar, and a scar tells a story of survival. A scar is attractive because it says, 'this man is tough and strong, he will protect you at all costs'."

"Hmmm…" He didn't sound convinced. Hell, she wasn't convinced by her own words. It wasn't really about the chair, or scars, or any other bullshit she might try to con herself with. She was drawn to him, unable to resist. She sighed.

"You think I will protect you at all costs?" His voice was a soft promise in her ear.

"Yes."

"I don't think you need protecting. You are brave, clever, and tough." A rush of noise filled her head. Not because she didn't believe him. She did. Because he saw the version of her that she wanted to be. She wanted to be brave. Perhaps she was in his eyes because he didn't know what she ran from.

"Enough about me, this house is huge for one person. Isn't it a bit greedy?" She deflected, poorly, away from herself.

"Nah. I designed it so whanau, family, could stay whenever they want. That whole half of the house—" He waved vaguely in the direction of the lift, "—is for them. There are three bedrooms, a bathroom, and guest living room over there."

"How do you clean it all?"

He laughed. "I pay someone. It's the benefit of being reasonably well off."

Thank fuck—he gave her something to rally against. A reason to deflect the topic away from herself. "How nice for you. My only indulgence is getting my suits dry cleaned."

"You'd be on a good salary though?"

"You know you aren't supposed to ask that." She pretended to laugh but he just raised his eyebrows. There was no getting past him. "Yeah, I do well enough, and I should get a good bonus cheque this year now that I'm on the Exec team."

"And yet you worry about cleaning? Get a cleaner, it's the best."

"I have a mortgage to pay. A Sydney sized mortgage."

"That's a bugger." He smirked and some of the tightness in her chest relaxed.

"You don't have a mortgage? What kind of charmed life do you lead?"

"I had a massive insurance payout."

Blood drained from her head, leaving her lightheaded. "Oh, shit. Sorry, I didn't think."

"Don't be sorry. I mean, initially I thought the price I paid was too high." He paused, giving her a considered stare, then he shrugged one shoulder in a tiny throw-away movement. "It didn't long for me to realise that I had to make the most of it."

"And now you swan around a mortgage free house living

the good life, with the ocean at your doorstep." She stared out the window at the dusky light playing over the sea, trying to slow the rapid beat of her heart. The sky had turned mauve, a backdrop with no clouds, and only a hint of sunset from behind the house, shards of coloured light slipping around the edges of her vision. She shivered as his fingers trailed along the edge of the blanket she had wrapped around her. It would be so easy to fall against his broad chest, to spend more time pressed against his dark, hot skin, to taste his salty masculine muscles. So very tempting.

"Stay with me." His whisper made her heart leap. Yes. No. She had a plan for her life. Where did he fit in that? She slid sideways on the couch, away from his touch, away from temptation. She tucked her knees up under the blanket, pulling it tight around her.

"You asked before if you bother me——" Her voice shook a little, cracked, and she licked her lips.

"You said yes. And I wonder if that was one of the first truly honest things you've told me." His brown eyes were liquid with concern, stopping her from flinching at his words.

"I've always been honest with you."

"Surface honesty. I meant a deep truth. I do bother you, and I want to know exactly why." Even his voice was warm with empathy, a level of caring that she'd only ever had from Sal before. It scared her. She suppressed a core deep shudder.

"The truth is——" The truth is that she didn't know why he bothered her. Was it because she felt truly comfortable with him? Was it the connection they had, a natural way of co-existing without effort? Yeah, that was it.

"—the truth is … I want you more than I want to want you." She babbled it out, staring at the wooden floor. He had no rugs in this house, nothing to soften the stark interiors, only the quirky collection of cushions he tucked around himself as he lounged on the couch, his eyes caressing her with his patience. Everything in this house looked outwards, towards the horizon, just as she always did. Wanting to achieve something rather than look inside at her problems. He shifted on the couch, a shuffle of cushions alerting her to glance at him.

"My architect told me to design this house for the future. That one day I might want to share it with a special someone, to fill it with a family. I told him he could do that if he wanted. No one was going to want the burden of my life." His eye twitched at the corner, like his eyes wanted to narrow, but he tried to stop them. She wanted to shake however thought he was a burden. If anything, she was the burden. "Back then, so soon after my accident, I didn't care to fight with them. Wiremu said the architect was right. I let them organise me because I was too busy working out how to get by each day, and too tired to argue with them."

"Oh." If that didn't tug her heartstrings, she didn't know what would. She'd never understood the cliché before now, until his words squeezed at her chest.

"I think I bother you … for the same reason the architect bothered me. You are so busy being brave, and simply getting by every day, that you don't plan for the future." His voice washed over her, the rounded vowels, the deep bass notes, they took away her reaction. *But I do plan for the future.* She swallowed. She planned for a future where she lived alone, controlled every aspect of her life, including her pleasure. She thought she'd wanted that life. A life where she didn't have to walk on eggshells in case she woke her mother from a drunken stupor and dished out random ugliness. A life without surprises. Fucking surprise—those wishes weren't the whole life she wanted at all. Not if she looked deep down in her heart at the desire she'd buried as a child. Tucked away so safe that she'd almost forgotten it was there. She'd always wanted a home, a home to be free and safe inside, one unburdened by disaster and instead, filled with love.

"Damn you." She let out a shaky breath. "Damn you and your fucking insights." He raised one eyebrow, a slight amused smirk hovered at the edge of his lip.

"Your secrets are safe with me. You are safe with me." It was a simple truth that ate away at her resistance.

"Ahh, don't make it sound so serious. It's not a secret. My mother, my fucking mother, loved to drink more than she loved me. When everything turned to shit, she drank, leaving me alone to figure it all out." And that's when she'd learnt to work, a necessity to look after herself. That's why she couldn't do this with Joey; because it would interfere with work, and thus her ability to have control and freedom.

"That sounds ... tough." Somehow, he managed to sound relieved.

"Sure. It's not something I'd wish on anyone. It's also not as awful as I bet you were imagining." She ran her tongue over her teeth as she tried to dismiss the conversation, hefting her shoulders in an exaggerated shrug.

He blinked once, presumably in agreement. "Yeah,

maybe. It still sounds awful to me. I grew up in a simple, lower middle class, loving home. Mum worked her butt off in dead end jobs to buy me boots. Dad took me to training. They spent hours on me. I can't imagine growing up without that commitment and easy knowledge that they love me."

She wrinkled her nose, pushing away the jealous flame that lit up inside when he mentioned his parents devoted love for him. Even before Baba had died, her parents had had a contentious relationship, and as an only child, she'd borne the brunt of their fights. She shrugged again. "I'm okay about it all. Everything was fine, typical family stuff, before Baba, that's what I called my Dad, died in a car crash when I was fifteen. Only after that did Mama start drinking seriously. Don't worry about me."

"I wouldn't dare worry about you."

"See. That's the problem with you, right there. I say something dismissive to make you stop prying. And you tell me I'm good enough already. It's an annoying comment that makes me want to tell everything." She tugged the blanket tighter.

"I have plenty of patience. You'll tell me when you are ready." With his head upright, and his hands held out palm up, he looked the picture of someone with all the time in the world, languid in repose, waiting for her. She stopped fighting the urge to run away. Maybe she could find a way to keep him compartmentalised, Joey in bed vs Joey at work. Oh, who was she kidding? Herself, that's who.

"It's complicated." A pathetic answer, but close enough to the truth. It shouldn't be complicated, this involvement with Joey, but somehow it had rapidly become complicated.

She didn't want to step away, the sex had been far too good to abandon, but these other responses she had around him made her want to restate her rules. Keep her distance for her own sake.

"Life is pretty complicated. People are complex, it's why they are so interesting."

"I didn't take you for the two-bit philosophy type." Her insides squirmed but she couldn't stop a smile from spreading. She almost pinched her lips together but stopped herself. Why shut down these moments of happiness? She could deal with the dread later.

"Nah, I read it on a meme." He held her gaze, deadpan, for a long moment. Laughter burst out, harder than she expected. She pressed her hand against her stomach.

"Good one." Her hands relaxed at his smile, broad and open. The blanket slipped off her shoulders. Cool air brushed her skin, and she shivered, tugging the blanket back up to cover herself.

"Are you cold? I'll warm you up if you stay the night."

Temptation rushed forwards again. Could she? She swallowed and looked around the room. Dusk had turned into the beginning of night. There was still enough light to see, although the bright colours of Sydney's summer faded into grey dull shadows. Somehow the lack of light made Joey appear more welcoming, the way the softened shadows lay on his face, highlighting his features, making his dark eyes shimmer like the ocean at night, tempting her to dive in and lose herself. Or become free from gravity, limbless and floating, supported by the water, supported by him. She couldn't do it. The ocean was full of dangerous creatures, she had to get out before these crashing emotions drowned her, or something big swallowed her up.

"I shouldn't. I need to get back to work. I've already had too much time away. Someone will have noticed." She made her excuses and started to stand up.

"Stay, get up early instead. I'm getting up early to go for a swim." His calm voice, deep and welcoming, made her relax back against the cushions.

"Where do you swim?"

"The Ian Thorpe Pool in the city."

"Isn't there an ocean pool at Coogee? That'd be lovely at this time of year." Ella gazed out over the almost dark ocean.

"There are three, but they aren't easily accessible." His calm acceptance of the matter made her sway. If it was her, she would demand change. Why shouldn't he be able to swim at his local beach's ocean pool? Her uncertainty about staying with him ebbed away, replaced by a growing tension in her veins.

"I don't have anything with me." She shrugged at the flimsy excuse, a barrier to stop her throwing herself at him for a hug.

"I can drop you at your place early on my way to the pools. Is before six okay?"

She sighed, a long slow sigh of submittal. She was really going to do this. "Yes, I'll stay. Then you can stop me from ringing the council and giving them a send-up about improving the access to Coogee's ocean pools."

He barked out a laugh. "You could still do that in the morning."

"I have enough to do without adding to my list. Perhaps I'll grab an Uber now."

"It's your choice. A no commitment offer to stay." He didn't even have the decency to look smug as he said the perfect thing. A rueful resignation washed over her, overtaking the steady drum of her heart at the idea of changing her routine. She could choose to stay, and she'd still be in control. She nodded, slow and hesitant.

12

Joey's gut relaxed at her agreement. He paused, wiping his clammy palms on his pants, his pulse had bounced with nerves as he waited for her answer. The easy way she'd dismissed his concerns told him that she often used that as a tactic to keep people away. She'd laughed, tightly, when mentioning abandonment issues, as if she wanted him to think she had all the answers, that she wasn't hurting. He wanted to wrap her in a hug and hold her safe. It had taken an inordinate control to keep to his end of the couch, and just let her be. Instead, he clapped his hands and the lights came on, flooding the room with light. Ella blinked under the onslaught, as she adjusted to the sudden light.

She grinned. "That's so cool."

"Yeah, it makes life heaps easier."

"What else can this house do?" She leaned slightly towards him. Was the light flush on her cheeks for him or his ability to purchase technology?

"Most of it is controlled from my phone, even the tv."

He pulled out his phone, opened the app, and turned on the tv.

"Holy fuck, that's super cool." He knew the wall slid back to reveal the tv, enjoying watching her reaction rather than the fun tech that he'd had built into his house. He liked that it was app-controlled, not through one of those internet devices, because he'd rather know what was happening to his data.

"Do you want something to drink, or is that the wrong thing to ask?" He scanned her face carefully in case she flinched. A micropause gave him the indication she hid a thought from him, so he looked at his phone to give her some space.

"It's fine. Shall I grab you something?" She leapt to her feet and walked to his kitchen, regal with his blanket draped down her back, dragging across his wooden floor.

"Yeah, there should be some beer in the fridge. I'm pretty sure there is some wine in the cupboard beside the fridge. The white won't be cold though." He flicked through the channels, not wanting to see her in his domestic space. He already had so much longing for her, he wanted to keep her here with him, to see her cook for him, and relax around him. He didn't want the image of her in his head where it might taunt him. They hardly knew each other, and he knew the longing came from how she responded so naturally to him and his chair. How she was one of the first people to make it a non-issue. Even his family had taken time to adjust. Not Ella, she saw him the way he saw himself, not to be pitied, but as someone who lived life with an obvious challenge. Many people had challenges in their life, most of them unseen, like Ella and her mother. He didn't see himself as any different to that; except that his change in circumstances was obvious. He'd heard all the noise people said about him, how it was a shame that a great athlete could be cut down. Nonsense. Retirement would've loomed soon enough, and he would've faded into obscurity. This way, he'd built something out of his injury. A life to be admired and enjoyed. The cushions on the couch shifted. His eyes flashed open in surprise as Ella sat beside him.

"Here you go." She passed him a beer, their fingers brushing, heat against the cool glass. "You look very serious. What are you thinking about?"

"Ahh—" Not anything he wanted to share, at least not precisely, "just a memory."

"Not a good one?" Placing a glass of orange juice on the coffee table, she twisted to face him. He pressed the tv app, changing it to music, so that his collection quietly filled the room with a random selection of tunes. The steady beat of Triple J's latest Hottest 100 album hummed out of the speaker system, a low undercurrent to his anticipation.

"I'm not sure if it's good or bad really."

Her eyebrows raised slowly. "Yeah?"

"When I was in the spinal unit, a young bloke arrived in the bed next to me. He made this cynical noise when he saw it was me, a laugh without humour. 'What?' I asked him. He said 'Joey Mananui? Mate, when you had your accident, I told my mates, that if it was me, I'd top myself. I couldn't imagine living life in a wheelchair.' I—"

"Fuck." She drew the word out into a long exclamation.

"I could've punched him, the fuckwit. What a thing to

say, and I'd only been there a month or so. I was so new on this journey, but I knew one thing. I wanted to live, and I didn't need this bullshit pity from some dickhead in the same place I was." He paused as she nodded, her teeth sinking into her lower lip.

"What did you do?"

He grinned at her shock because he'd done that on purpose. "I didn't do anything. Because you know what he said next?"

"What?"

"What a fucking idiot I am. I'd rather be alive in a chair, than fucking dead."

She gasped, then slowly a giggle escaped. She clamped her hand over her mouth as if she was embarrassed to laugh at his story. "Oh my god. That shouldn't be funny, but fuck."

"Pretty much. Paul is an amazing guy. He broke his C6 and has almost no movement at all below his neck, yet he's just built his third app and is making mega-bucks. And he's the funniest dickhead you'll ever meet."

"That's quite special." Ella's face sobered as she spoke.

"What do you mean? People shouldn't have to be exceptional in order to be seen as human." He sipped his beer. Even though he'd been able to trust her empathy, not pity, so far, he had enough experience with being the inspiring stereotype that he automatically assumed her next comment would be ignorant and maybe hurtful.

"I didn't mean that. I spend my life with workaholics, people with massive drive, handpicked by Vince to sell the world to itself, people who only care for financial success. People around me burn out, and fade away, and the rest of us trample on them to get higher. It can be ugly, especially when I'm one of them. Stories like that make me wonder if I've chosen the right path." She sighed, her breath fluttering beside him.

"Everyone has their own challenges, and their own talents. I'm sure it's not as brutal as you make it sound." He wanted to keep her talking about herself because she usually deflected away and he yearned to know more. He checked to make sure his mouth wasn't hanging open.

"Nah, it's worse." Her smile hovered between enjoyment and a sneer.

"Do you regret it?"

"Mostly, no. I like the consistency of it." She twisted her long hair around her hand.

"And arguing?"

She nodded, an amusement sparkling in her eyes. "Legal arguments are all about structure, I like the rhythm of it, the puzzle unravelling. My only regret is being part of a system that benefits the current power holders. I thought that choosing to be outside the legal system itself and instead working in business as an advisor wouldn't be like that. Now I'm not so sure." She paused, waving her hand ruefully.

"I hope you aren't having second thoughts because of me."

She waggled her head side to side, as if weighing it up. "What would old Quong say? Is this the legacy he'd want?"

"You told me he was a businessman. I reckon he'd be proud of you."

"Thanks." She let out a long breath. "There's a good chance you're right. I reckon he might be proud of me. I'm the first person of Chinese descent on the Exec team, and the first woman. It's crazy to think, because I don't feel very Chinese, our family has been here for so many generations, I've never been to China, but I still look Chinese. Well, you must know this, how people judge what they can see."

"Yeah." Light-headedness made his fingers tighten around his beer. No wonder she saw past his chair to him. She understood being judged on appearance. If he wasn't careful, he was going fall in love with her. It'd be a crash he'd never recover from, especially if she kept running away from him.

"People assumed I'd become a wheelchair athlete. Wiremu gets emails from teams all the time, wanting me to join up." Worry nagged at him, sending a cold chill over his skin and making the hair on his forearms rise up, as her comments about her career brought up the question of whether she was here to benefit from his fame. It had roared when she mentioned trampling on others to further her career and hadn't gone away as she'd discussed her own doubt about whether her career choices were the right ones. Probably just habit; she hadn't really shown that to him, it just came from a long history of people wanting to benefit from his fame and fortune.

"Why don't you join?" She pursed her lips, a wrinkle of a frown between her fine brows. His hand gripped his beer, taut, at the suggestion that he continue his glory days as an athlete. He opened his mouth to protest, when she said, "No, scratch that thought. The frown on your face tells me you aren't interested in their offers. Why not?"

"I'd probably be good at whatever sport they want. It's

not about that. I just don't want to spend my whole life defined as an athlete." He sipped the cool beer, the carbonation a perfect swirl against his tongue, the taste of relaxation, in opposition to the tightness building in his chest.

"But you are literally the face of inclusion at sport with the new deal your agent did with us at Kapow?" Her cheeks were painted with a light flush. "… Everyone ends up being defined somehow. Isn't it best to be remembered for your passion, for something you care about?" She leaned forward and picked up her glass. The blanket draped around her body parted as she reached, gifting him with the perfect view of her cleavage and the tantalising hint of ink under her breast. A hint that disappeared as she leaned back to sip her juice. He held his breath as she replaced the glass on the table, that touch of ink peeking out again from the blanket as she leaned forward once more. He lost track of their conversation, his mind blank.

"Is that why you got your tattoo? Because you are defined by your job?" Joey's mild curiosity about the inky words under her breast surged into mind-blowing desire in a second as she flicked the blanket back, and traced her finger along the tattoo, her hand curving with the shape of her exposed breast. His eyes felt like they'd bug right out. Holy fucking hell, this woman would be the death of him. He pounced, throwing himself at her, torso first in a wild lunge, his arms wrapped around her as he pressed himself against her temptation. His half-full beer slipped out of his hand and bounced on the hard floor.

"Joey!" She shrieked. "Have you lost your mind?" Her body burned against his skin, her soft feminine form anchored under him. He gripped the edge of the couch and started to lift himself off her at her tone.

"Have you? Fuck, Ella. You can't just thrust your boobs at me and expect no response." Cool air sent a shiver down his body as he drew himself off her. Shock at his reaction to her baiting him mixed in his guts with disgust at his lack of control. His biceps and shoulders ached as he struggled to shift off her. Later he could call himself an idiot, right now he had to fix this.

She smiled, her eyes dancing. "I can if I get a response like this."

He blinked at the disarming notion that she'd wanted his reaction. "Are you trying to drive me wild?"

Her smile extended further, and she ducked her head sideways. She nipped at his earlobe, shots of heat and need flashed over his skin. Her arms wrapped around him, pulling him against her, until he was sinking, lost to reason. They kissed, lips finding each other in frantic need, tongues battling for mutual pleasure. The familiarity of her taste hummed in his veins, his heart beating strong with knowledge of her, of the utter gift she gave him. Complete acceptance of who he was now. He reached up and cradled her face, tucking a stray strand of hair behind her ear. That cheeky earring of hers, the one at the top of her ear, was all out of place against her often spouted wish for control. A rebellious choice for someone so obsessed with order. Or maybe…

"You did this to get your mother's attention, didn't you?"

Her eyes flashed open. "Enough with the character analysis. For Christ's sake, can we just fuck?"

"Maybe in a while." He brushed his thumb down the edge of her ear, as she wriggled under him. To entice, not escape. "Shhhh. You don't have to do drastic things to get my attention."

"Don't be so fucking arrogant. Get off me, and take me to bed, properly." Her wide grin gave away her faked fury. He kissed her hard on the mouth, a no-holds barred kiss, her taste, sweet and tart like a crisp apple, seared onto his tongue as he gave her everything she asked for. Desperate sex that took them both to a place where they didn't have to think.

"Who needs a bed for that?"

13

Ella cracked one eye open as the bright electronic beeps of an alarm sang out. The first shards of sunrise pierced the night sky, a red glow on the horizon over a flat sea. A groan rumbled through the bed. Oh shit. Joey. She blinked away her sleep, trying not to dwell on the fact that she'd actually spent the night, all night, with Joey.

"I guess if I'm going to break all my rules, I may as well do them spectacularly."

"What did you say?" Joey murmured against her back. Fuck, did she say that aloud?

"Nothing. Just complaining because morning is here too fast." She started to slip out of bed, halted by his arm wrapping around her waist.

"I could give up my swim and have a different form of exercise."

A sense of intrigue washed over her body. She'd never had wake up sex before. He caressed his hand along her side, down over her hips, warm on her sleep heavy skin. The sheer intimacy of it all shocked her wide awake. She bolted out of bed, her feet hitting the cool wooden floor.

"You could. But I really have to go to the office. Everyone will be wondering where I went yesterday." She stood still, staring out the windows at the vast ocean. The spectacular sight of the sun rinsing the ocean with painted red, yellow, and orange streaks held her static, entranced. Only the buzz of a growing list of tasks at the back of her skull forced to her move. She gathered up her clothes, still scattered around the room from yesterday's exertions. Her wrinkled suit lay ruined on the floor, one arm of her jacket inside out. God, they'd been frantic, only her shoes were neatly tucked beside the bed, everything else flung far and wide. The glory of it, their uncontrolled need for each other, now rammed home. Somehow seeing her shoes perfectly neat together beside his bed made the lack of control worse, building as a panic in her clenched stomach.

"Don't worry about getting up. I'll just get an Uber." She threw on her clothes, slightly frantic with her fingers trembling as she finished the buttons on her jacket until she brushed down the front, although only a drycleaner and a good press could rid it of those wrinkles.

"I'm coming." His sleepy voice rumbled, a timbre of gravel that filled her with wonder. She'd never understood that expression of gravel in a man's voice until now. She closed her eyes and let out a long slow breath. Perhaps she should use the calming exercises she often used before going into a tense business meeting. The soft rustle of bed sheets, the quiet rhythm of his breath, invaded her peace.

"It's going to be a hot one again today."

Her eyes flicked open to see him roll past her into the bathroom, leaving her alone to face the onslaught on the sun. He was right. Already you could feel the heat in the summer sun as it rose, those prickly shards of heat. Thankfully, she'd be in her airconditioned office all day. Shit. She needed to shower, get a new suit. No wonder she was out of sorts, there was nothing worse than the icky feeling of old clothes on a new morning. She sighed at her own melodrama. Of course, there were worse things than old clothes. Much worse and it didn't take much digging in her memory to know a few of them.

"Bathroom is all yours now. I'll meet you downstairs if you like." Joey's words jerked her properly awake. How long had she stood there, uncertain?

"Sure. Thanks." Her voice was tight and high-pitched. How could he act like this was so normal? To get up and begin the day with someone he hardly knew. She pressed her hands against her stomach to ward off the quiver of doubt. What had she let herself into? She spun around, the sun warm on her back, to see him roll away, already clothed. She shook out her hands, paced to the bathroom and splashed her face with cold water. The cool refreshing liquid hit her face, snapping her back into the world. She rolled her shoulders, then reached up and ran her fingers through her hair. Little knots had formed at the back of her neck, where her hair had rubbed against the pillows, and she tugged them apart.

She walked towards the lift on hesitant steps, deliberately slowing her breathing to calm her elevated pulse. How weird to be nervous now? She'd already shared her body with

Joey and loved every moment. Somehow, the act of leaving the house together added an extra level of importance that she felt ill-equipped to deal with. The doors slid open, and she walked inside. Pressing the button reminded her of all the items of her to-do list this week, and calm returned to her chest as the lift slipped down into the basement, the sharp heat of the sun disappearing. Stop over-reacting to all this, and just get to work where everything is ordered.

Fifteen minutes later, the car roared up the short driveway and onto the street. Ella glanced at Joey who drove with a slight grin on his face, his simple enjoyment of life making her feel like a fool for worrying so much. If he could find happiness in a growly engine, she could also take on the simple pleasures of life without all this thinking.

"My place is in Surry Hills, it's just a unit, nothing special," she said.

"Pretty nice spot to have an apartment, though. Do you have a favourite place to eat around there?"

She shrugged. "How do you pick? There are heaps of good places."

"Super. How about I drop you off, and we meet for breakfast once you've done all that stuff that women do in the mornings?"

"You mean like shower, and wear clean clothes?" She chuckled as he winked at her. "You'll be the death of my career. I can't afford any more time with you. I already wasted a whole afternoon yesterday."

"Not a waste." Joey's tone was clipped and it stabbed at her chest.

"Shit. I didn't mean it like that." She glanced, hesitant,

at him, only to see his grin stretching wide across his handsome face. Her fingers twitched in her lap, the idea of tracing along those high cheekbones, to feel his breath on her skin.

"I know what you meant." The confidence in his voice made her smile back at him. She brushed her hand over the back of his, as it rested on the steering wheel, a quick thanks for his reassuring belief in her. The zing as she touched him made her snatch her hand back into her lap. Perhaps she wasn't at all assured by where this was going.

The corner of his mouth twitched. "I want you to eat something this morning, you can't do all that work on an empty stomach."

"I'll be fine. I always grab coffee and a bite to eat on the way to the office." She thumbed open her phone and flicked through emails. The steady thrum of the car engine mixed with the irregular beat of the tunes on the radio.

"Oh my goodness. How delightful!" One email made her smile, a soft, happy smile, perfect to sooth her frantic wave of emotion that Joey created.

"What?" He kept his eyes on the road. A song ended, and the news flowed through the radio. A slow news day with a rubbish story about some c-grade celebrity that she'd never heard of.

"Just my friend Sal, and her wild Nana's antics. She's been giving all the staff at her nursing home grief." Ella continued to flick through her emails, the one from Sal providing relief from the constant work, work, work. Before meeting Joey, she'd wanted that life more than anything else. Suddenly it seemed unfulfilling to be so singularly focused on her career. She blinked, now who was being ridiculous. This was just a bit of fun, nothing serious. Good sex, that was all.

After navigating the roads between Coogee and Surry Hills, they pulled up out the front of her building.

"Traffic is pretty sweet at this time of day." She did enjoy the way Joey had driven in silence, listening to his tunes, so she could organise her workday. It was a peaceful habit, one she appreciated if she didn't think too hard about how they coexisted so easily. She checked the mirror, opened the door and stepped out of the car, swinging her bag onto her shoulder.

Her tenant, Etienne called out from the pavement. "Hey Ms Tart, the tap in the bathroom is dripping again." She'd bought the unit next door last year, but it was plagued with maintenance problems. Thankfully her tenant was good humoured about it.

"Good morning Etienne. I can get someone to fix that for you today, if that will work for you." Just another task to add to her long list, but one she didn't mind. She liked the responsibilities that came with being a landlord, they gave her a sense of control over her own destiny. Yes, she needed the reminder from Etienne to keep her life on target. She had goals, and good sex couldn't derail those.

"Thanks. And by the way, your boyfriend has a cool car. Do you think he'll let me drive it one day?"

"He's not my—" She stopped herself mid-denial. "I doubt it." She grinned at her tenant, then spun around on her dainty heels towards Joey. He leaned out the window, and she planted a firm kiss direct on his lips. Having goals for her life didn't mean she couldn't own the assumption. Boyfriend sounded pretty damned good in the warm sunshine. Her stomach flipped over, caught between her old goals and the newness of being with Joey.

"Have a lovely day, Joey." She walked away before he could react, and once inside, she bolted to her unit. She dumped her phone on the kitchen counter and stripped off yesterday's clothes. A scalding shower bit into her skin, washing away all the events of the day before, the steam clearing her lungs until she emerged from the water, dripping and free again. The simple routine of her morning began, bringing an unthinking normality to her day. The time with Joey faded away, into a dreamlike memory, except for the niggling worry that he'd imbedded himself in her heart.

With her hair dry and her attire suitably precise, Ella walked back into her tiny lounge-kitchen area to unpack her bag and reorganise it for the day. Her phone dinged.

Joey: Was that your flatmate?

Ella: My tenant.

Joey: If you own the unit and they pay you rent. Isn't that like a flatmate?

Ella: What does it matter?

Joey: I'm curious.

Ella: Jealous?

Ella paused, her thumbs hovering over the keypad. Oh, what did it matter? She'd already shared so much with him…

Ella: I own the unit next to mine too. Etienne is my tenant.

Joey didn't respond, those little dots that indicated he

was typing showed up, but no message arrived. She quite liked the idea of his potential jealousy. Still, her tenants were none of his business. Curiosity won the battle over dismissal.

Ella: It doesn't make me rich, just indebted.

Joey: Part of your need to succeed?

Ella: Nothing wrong with ambition! Anyway, I've gotta get to work. Chat later?

She shoved the phone in her bag, so she wouldn't see the notifications if he answered, and stalked out of the door. Today she was determined to stick to her old goals; and she tried to ignore the little voice in her head that told her she could have both. Goals and Joey. No, life had taught her she had to be independent in order to be free from emotional pain.

14

Ella stared at her lounge. It'd been a few weeks since she'd slept here, and the place had garnered a dusty disused air. She threw open the windows, to let in fresh air, or at least, an attempt to let in some air. The still, hot, Sydney summer air didn't move inside, it only hovered at the fringes. She'd spent almost every spare moment in the past three weeks with Joey, and they'd fallen into an easy routine. Up early, he went to the pool to swim, and she went to the office. Every few days, she'd come back here in her lunch-break to do laundry, swap over dry cleaning, and re-pack her bags. Without even realising it, she'd slowly been leaving things at his house. The weight of that hit her as she stood in her baking lounge, dust tickling her nose.

She had a few hours to fill in before the welcoming dinner for Kapow's new client. All their global brand management team had arrived in Sydney and they'd spent the day running over Kapow's plans for their new direction.

As the lawyer, she hadn't been required to speak during the day, except to answer a few minor questions about discrimination law. She'd avoided meeting Joey's eyes all day as he performed his part in the reveal. Dinner would be different; she would have to navigate her burgeoning relationship with Joey in public. The act of standing in her house made her realise just how much she'd allowed her life to flow into his. When she was with him, it happened naturally. One touch was all it took. Every time. She plumped up the pillows on the couch, sneezing quietly once, then settled herself down with legs tucked under her body. Her phone rang. She leapt up to grab it from the kitchen counter.

"Hey Sal." How long had it been since she'd spoken to her best friend?

"You must be busy, yeah? I haven't heard from you in almost three whole weeks." Sal's familiar tones swept away the weight pressing on her chest.

"Do you want to come over for a catch up?" She should have rung Sal for a chat before now.

"Yeah, sure. I'll be there in twenty. Want me to bring anything?" A note of false bravado coloured Sal's tone.

"What's the matter?" Suddenly none of her problems mattered as Sal's breath shook in her ear.

"It can wait until I get there."

Ella waited as Sal breathed quietly into the phone twice before the connection was cut off. After slipping on some sandals, she grabbed her purse and headed out to grab some snacks and a bottle of wine for Sal. Time spent with her best mate would be exactly what she needed. Maybe she could work out how her life had become entangled with Joey's so quickly, so deeply entangled that she hadn't talked to her best friend for weeks. A faintly bitter taste coated her tongue.

The smell of summer fruits lingered in the air as the buzzer rang twenty minutes later. She smiled at Sal's face in the tiny screen and pressed the button to let her in the building. Soon enough, a knock banged on the door, and she opened it with arms outstretched for Sal.

"Hey, doll. It's been forever, and you never go this long without calling me." Sal stepped back, her hands still resting on Ella's shoulders. Ella's face blossomed with heat.

"Oh. Well, fuck me. It's a bloke."

Ella felt her face explode into an inane grin. "Yip."

Sal marched to the couch, plonking herself down. She picked up the wine bottle, twisted off the cap, and poured for both of them in the two glasses Ella had put on the table earlier. Sal was the only person in the world that Ella would drink with. She knew the whole sorry tale about her mother, and Ella trusted her to help keep her necessary boundaries.

"Tell me everything." Sal stretched out the last word and raised both eyebrows. Ella paused, compiling her thoughts until the perfect phrase popped out. "This is pretty much your fault. You told me to enjoy my time with Joey—"

"Joey, the rich, hot, league player that you've lusted over forever. The one you nervously spoke to me about before a one night stand? I take it your quiet afternoon drinks were just the start of things?" Sal held out her glass. Ella clinked hers together, a hint of the oaky tannin scent of the Hunter

Valley Merlot rising up to add to the celebration. On the rare occasion she did partake in a little wine, she always wished she didn't have to worry so much. The divine taste on her tongue was other-worldly.

"Tell me everything, darl." Sal repeated herself. Ella opened her mouth – where to start? – then changed tact.

"First … tell me why you rang tonight? What's the matter?" She sipped the wine, the earthy flavour on her tongue as Sal's face tightened.

"Nana is ill." Three little words. How could such a small phrase punch her in the chest?

Ella rested her hand over Sal's. "I'm sorry." Only three weeks ago, Sal had sent an email about Nana's feisty arguments with the staff. Had she gone downhill so fast?

"It's fine. I mean, it's not, but she is, like, ninety." Sal's breath shook.

"Remember that time I came over for Christmas?" Ella filled the long silence with her favourite story about Sal's Nana.

"OMG – I'd forgotten that. And Ricki gave me a rechargeable torch! Fucking funniest thing ever."

"His face when Nana said 'is that one of those things you use in the bedroom?' I've never seen a deeper shade of pink." Ella shook her head. Sal giggled once, a hiccup of a laugh. Tears started to stream down her face. Ella gently took Sal's glass, placed it on the table and gathered her friend into a hug. Sobs shook Sal's body as Ella stroked Sal's back, soothing the gulping depths of sadness, her own face wet with tears. Sal's Nana was generous, open-minded. She'd always opened her house and her heart to Ella, a gift of family when her own family became too much to bear. She might never have survived after Baba's death if it wasn't for Sal and Nana. Her own heart ached, for her friend, and for Nana.

"It's bone cancer, they say—" Sal's words came out clear. "Doctors say she only has a few weeks left."

"Shit. I have a work function tonight, but I can cancel if you need."

"No, you go to your thing. Maybe—"

"Let's visit tomorrow. Nothing is more important than this." Ella closed her eyes and ran through her to-do list. Today's meeting had ended with a bazillion action points. Everything could be moved to make Sal and Nana her priority.

"Thank you."

"No problem. How is Ricki doing?"

Sal sucked in a deep breath that ended with a shake. "You know him. He's being the righteous big brother. He doesn't think I should have any say in what happens next because I'm—"

"Going to hell?" Ella leapt in before Sal had a chance to say lesbian. The tone Ricki used for that word made it into an insult, rather than the simple description it should be.

"Yeah."

"Goddamn family." Ella picked up her wine, gulping some down. "I'd rather be in hell with you, than in his boring slice of heaven."

Sal smiled, a hesitant flicker of her lips. "Nana will be with us too."

"When I grow up, I want to be like Nana. She never bothered with anyone's bullshit."

"I'm going to miss her."

"Don't say that. We are going to visit tomorrow. And we won't tell anyone because it should be just the three of us." Ella planned to block all the entranceways, so her best friend could spend time alone with her Nana without anyone else, especially Sal's uptight bigoted brother Ricki, interfering.

"I'll drink to that." Sal swigged down her glass of wine, an angry emotional gulp that made the hair on the back of Ella's neck rise up.

"Maybe slow down a little."

"This would be easier if Ricki—"

"—wasn't a judgemental idiot." Ella finished Sal's sentence for her again. She sipped her wine. "I'm sorry, he's your brother and all, but really, most Christians are more open-minded to the world than that. How on earth did your parents, and Nana, create him?"

"We've had this discussion before. He was just born like that. I think he likes the constancy of the church, the idea of faith and forgiveness sit well with him."

"Makes sense. I guess when your parents are successful creative types, there isn't much routine that happens at home."

"No different to your situation though."

Ella waved her hand and shrugged. They'd been over this discussion many times. "Never mind all that. What do you reckon Nana will say about Joey?" Ella would miss Nana's advice, and if there was one thing in her life she needed advice about right now, it was how to cope with Joey taking over her life.

"Are you kidding me? She's been a Dragons fan forever. You want to date a Tigers player? She's going to lose her shit!" Sal's eyes widened and she waved her wine in front of her, so the rich red liquid sloshed up the edge of the glass.

"True. Maybe it's best not to excite her?"

Sal shoved her in the shoulder. "You always fall for that!" She threw her head back and cackled. A forced laugh underpinned with fragility.

"Excuse me?" Ella blinked, confused by the sudden joviality and Sal's jest.

"Darl, I bet Nana would love to meet him. You know she follows all the young, hot players every year." Sal's wet eyes crinkled at the edges as she grinned.

"How did we go from asking Nana what she'd say, to meeting him?" Ella asked cautiously. Once she introduced Joey to Nana, then it would another step towards their relationship meaning more than sex. As it was, she'd already become lost in her time with him and forgotten to ring her best friend. Nauseous bile stung the back of her throat. What on earth was she doing?

"Wouldn't it be the best present though? To meet one of the greats of the game in her dying days?" Sal dragged in a shaky breath and brushed away more tears. Ella leapt up to grab a box of tissues and passed them to Sal, who blew noisily. It would be a great present, and a wonderful way to thank Nana for all her support and love. If only it didn't come with a big 'but'… But he might think Ella really cared for him? But wouldn't it make them officially together? But what if she'd already fallen for him? No, she hadn't. She could compartmentalise this. Her pulse skipped a beat. Sure.

"I'll ask him."

"You don't sound convinced."

Ella sipped her wine, taking her time to let the liquid round in her mouth, "If I'm honest…"

"Always a good plan."

"Hey, I never lie to you."

"I know, babe. Sometimes you lie to yourself, though. We all do." Sal poured herself more wine.

"True. The problem is that it's going too well. We hardly ever argue, except when it's fun to argue. I tell him stuff that I've only ever told you…" Another sip of wine slipped down Ella's tight throat.

"The sex?"

"Is amazing."

Sal clinked her glass and they both drank again. "Where exactly is the problem?"

"It's too intense, too fast. I haven't spent any time in this house for three weeks, since we met."

"Sounds pretty normal for the start of a relationship to me."

"What if it fades? How can it possibly keep up at this intensity?" The burr in her throat tickled, and she drank another sip to swallow it away.

"Doll. Alicia and I have been together for what … eight years now. Yes, the intensity at the beginning fades, the 'can't keep your hand off each other' moments don't last. That frantic need to be in each other's pants slows and ebbs with time. It's not a bad thing. It's normal."

Ella nodded cautiously. "Okay?"

"Do you talk to each other? Or is it just manic sex?"

"Both! He has this way about him. I just want to tell him everything, and it spews out. The other night, we were lying on the couch as the dusk faded. He read a novel, while I—"

Sal interrupted with a grin. "—he's reads? And he's an animal in bed. Tell me why you are worried?"

"I'm being ridiculous, aren't I?" Ella hiccupped. The confusion raging in her head during this discussion made her woozy. She placed her glass on the table, with a slight rattle as it hit the table harder than she intended.

"No. Doubt is normal."

"But?" Ella saw Sal refill her glass, a vague notion that she should pay attention to the quantity appeared then faded like an early morning fog covering the ocean. She trusted Sal.

"The really cool thing about a relationship is that the frantic need is slowly replaced with a deep love." Sal had the utter confidence of someone in a long term loving relationship.

"How do I figure out if this is going that way?"

"Do you like him?"

"Excuse me?" Ella sipped her wine, letting the oaky flavours sit on her tongue as she tried to understand the question. Of course, she liked him. "Oh. Oh, I think I get what you mean. It's more than lust, or fandom, or admiration..."

"Yeah, how about just plain liking? Do you enjoy his

company when you aren't in bed? Do you find his thoughts interesting? Does he listen? Is he likeable?"

"You want me to distil this down into compartments?" Ella screwed her eyes shut as she tried to figure it out. She couldn't—not when she wanted to keep Joey over there in the great sex department—nowhere else in her life. She couldn't afford to risk loving someone. She opened her eyes to peer at Sal who winked.

"No. You already know what you feel about him. You can't put emotions into a spreadsheet to keep them in line."

Ella rolled her eyes. "I don't particularly like spreadsheets."

"Who does?" Sal shrugged.

"Accountants, I suppose? I quite like getting my statements from them. All those numbers all lined up saying how much I earned." She gulped the wine, a drop sloshing down onto her thumb. "Shit. What were we talking about?"

"Joey?"

"Oh, fuck. Dinner with the new client. I have to get ready." Ella stood up, wobbling on her feet. Her blood rushed to her toes and she had to pause, blinking, as the world swirled and wavered. She tucked her chin against her neck and took a hesitant step towards her bedroom. Each step made the disconcerting lack of balance disappear and evolve into confidence. A niggling feeling made her turn around. Sal sat hunched over, her shoulders still heaving. Suddenly, her concerns about Joey and where this … situation with him might be headed dissolved. Her friend was in pain. That was all that mattered. She rushed over, and wrapped Sal into a hug.

"Oh God, what am I going to do once Nana dies?" Sal's voice was shaky, her breath broken.

"How about we figure that out later? All we can do is spend time with her until then." Ella had only happy memories of Nana, who had provided a safe, happy place for the two of them when the world had been mean to their angsty teenage selves.

"You'll organise Joey to meet her, yeah?"

"Yes. I promised." Even as she spoke, Ella knew it might be a white lie. She baulked at the idea of asking him to go back to his past. He might get paid to talk about it, his glorious career, the accident, and his inspirational new life, but he avoided questions about it when it was just the two of them. Somehow she wondered if the speaking was the sanitised version, and there was a deeper truth that he hid from everyone. Was it the fandom he hated? Or did he still grieve for his past? It was lucky she wasn't in love with him, or the answers to these questions would really matter. But she'd promised Sal—her best friend—so she'd find a way. Sal sat up straight, and Ella's arm slid around her shoulders.

"Shall we toast Nana?"

"Absolutely." Ella filled their glasses with an enthusiastic slop and passed one to Sal. They clinked and drank.

"To Nana. May her amazing sense of humour live on through us."

"Nana. I hope to be as kind to our grandkids as she was to us."

"Oh my god, isn't she the best! I can't believe how often we lounged at her place with the worries of the world, and all she did was offer us tea and cookies."

"And a smile. 'You are brave, Ella. This will pass,' she would say." Ella sipped her wine, not tasting it anymore.

"She'd be pretty mad at us, sitting here crying over her. For Christ's sake, Sal, pull yourself together. I'm not fucking dead yet." Sal imitated Nana's voice perfectly, and Ella's gulp of wine caught in her throat. She coughed as Sal slapped her on the back.

15

Ella sat quietly through most of the work dinner, conversation flowing around her. She'd tiptoed out of the Uber, her head still fuzzy with Sal's grief, and the couple of glasses of wine they'd shared. Somehow that bottle had been empty when she'd left for this dinner, hopefully Sal had drunk most of it, hopefully she hadn't had more than two glasses. Her woozy head gave her the inkling of a clue that she hoped against hope. Stu sat at the other end of the table, with Joey, Muhit, and the other men who worked for their new client. A few of their client's employees had brought their wives, a good chance for a holiday in sunny Sydney, and the women had congregated at this end, chatting to each other while enjoying the expensive dinner at one of Sydney's nicest hotels overlooking Hyde Park.

Ella toyed with a glass of white wine during dinner, unable to focus enough to stop the waiter pouring some for her. The group of women were fascinating, a diverse group and most of them were successful career women in their own rights, and yet happy to tag along with their husbands on a trip to Australia. It was also nice to not be the only Asian person at the table. Ella couldn't see herself as making the same choice, even though the parallel was obvious. She didn't want to admit that these women were showing her the life she could have with Joey if she stopped fretting about all the ways it could go wrong.

"I hate those ads where women are with hopeless men. Just leave him if he's so useless. Find a decent bloke who will help around the house. God, it's modern society now, roles are shared."

"Yeah, I read somewhere that men who do chores get more sex." The group giggled.

"You should say that louder, so they can all hear." A gorgeous Black woman nodded towards the men at the other end of the table.

Ella toyed with her dessert, pushing the rich chocolate cake around the plate. How was it that everything came back to Joey? That first kiss, his smooth cocoa taste on her mouth, the way he devoured her. She took a small bite, the pistachio crunch on top creating the perfect combination with the cake. Voices rang across the table, people getting more enthusiastic in their discussions as they imbibed freely on the Kapow purse-strings.

"Anyone want a whisky to finish?" Stu called out over everyone, as he stood up and waved at the waitress.

"Sure." Ella added her agreement to the suggestion. She'd already drunk more this afternoon with Sal than she had in the last decade, what harm would one more do?

"What are you doing?" Joey hissed, and she jerked her

head to see him beside her. Damn those wheels and his silent gliding.

"Partaking in a social ritual," she sneered. It was none of his business what she did.

"You don't drink. And for good bloody reason. Are you mad?"

"No, I'm not fucking angry." She whispered back at him. "You don't control me. You don't get to tell me what I can and can't do."

He blinked once, then glared at her. "Forgive me for caring." Of course, it was that moment that the whole fucking table decided to stop talking. His single comment, the one that told everyone about them, drifted into the silent pause. Every head turned and stared at them. Ella's face exploded with heat, her cheeks stinging with embarrassment.

"You aren't my husband yet. Leave me alone." She leapt to her feet, her chair clanging on the floor as it tipped over. The whispers started, whizzing around the table.

"OMG, are they sleeping together?" Was that Craig's voice? She stormed out of the room with terror buzzing in her ears. To where? To nowhere. Anywhere but here. Fast. She pushed her way out of the hotel front door, and ran, stumbled down the stairs. The world outside was blurry. Shit, tears made everything foggy. Or was that just her head?

"Wait." Joey's voice rang out from behind her. She spun around, reaching out for the handrail as she wobbled.

"No. You wrecked everything."

"Stop. Please."

"Do I need to spell it out for you? My career matters. I

was doing a good job in there, and you had to ruin it by announcing us to everyone." Her lungs screamed for air, in complete contrast to the gentle way he rolled down the side ramp towards her. His brown eyes glittered with danger.

"I believe you did an excellent job of that announcement yourself." He sounded so rational, she wanted to thump him.

"You didn't have to taunt me into it. Fuck, Joey."

He grabbed her hand. "Come with me." His calm tone only riled up the buzzing in her veins.

"Where?" She tugged her hand away, "I mean, No."

"This way." He reached out, using his strength to pull her onto his lap. Her skin came alive as she landed on him.

"What have you done to me?" She clung to his neck, her face wet against his collar.

"Ella, what have you done to yourself?" His breath was hot and heavy on her hair and she had only the faintest knowledge that he was taking her somewhere. Away from an embarrassing situation. Had she seriously called him her husband? She'd buried that wish deep down until now. That's it. She was never going to touch a drop of alcohol again. Wine was a curse that had ruined her life many times over. She should have known better than to let herself end up here. Like this. In a dramatic, drunken flounce out of a business dinner. Damn it all to hell. Everything she'd ever feared had happened.

"A room please." Joey's voice caressed her and she tried to bury herself against him, letting out a shuddery breath. She'd never get enough of him. She wanted a brutal orgasm, to feel him on her skin for the rest of the week. She needed to be taken away from the mess of her life. It was his fault… Her fault… No, he ruined the dinner by announcing their relationship to the room—not in as many words, but fuck— her career was on the line here. Yet she still craved him. What a mess.

"Punish me." She whispered into his ear, hot and desperate to throw away this unabandoned feeling of rage and confusion. The unsteadiness that came from way too much alcohol. Joey was safe, a haven from the riot in her head and chest.

"Thank you, sir." Joey spoke to someone else, ignoring her plea. Ella squeezed her eyes tight, wanting to be anywhere but here, curled up in his lap, drunken confusion whirling in her brain. She registered, faintly, that Joey was moving again, rolling, taking her somewhere.

"Doors closing." For a second, she thought they were on a train, but that made no sense. She flickered her eyes open. Oh, a lift. One of those annoying talking lifts.

"I've heard it said that someone's real personality comes out when they are drunk." Joey's voice breathed over her hair.

"Are you saying that I'm a reckless bitch?" Ella leapt out of his lap, light-headed and swaying, and stared him with her hands on her hips. She blinked hard to keep him in focus.

He grinned at her. "I didn't make any judgements."

Her chest heaved, as her breath panted in and out. She squinted at him. Why were they here? Oh, that's right. "I'm not a child. I can't believe you told everyone about us, and then bundled me in here like a baby in your lap."

"Like a baby?" Joey's eyebrows rose impossibly high.

"Yeah, like a little fucking baby who can't control themselves. I'm in complete control—" She sucked in a deep breath, "—of my life. I don't need some big noting famous guy to use his famous points to take that away." Did she just say famous twice? It rang around her head like a chant. Famous, famous, famous, until she had to squeeze her eyes tight to make it go away.

"Famous points? Where are you going with this, Ella?"

Her eyes flew open, and she pointed her finger at him, faintly registering the tension in his voice. The rage in her veins, fuelled by Sal's wine, dominated over caution. "You. You have all the power in this relationship." She spat out that last word, throwing all her frustration into it. "And I have nothing. Not anymore. The one thing that mattered to me—having my life under control. It's all a mess now."

"And you think I took that away from you?" Joey rolled backwards, his eyes not leaving hers as the lift doors slid open.

"Yes." Deep down she knew that wasn't fair, but when was any part of this fair? "It's not fair." Ella marched down the hallway, following him, rage whispering at him.

"And you said you aren't a child. You sure sound like a petulant child." Joey swiped a card and pushed open the door to a hotel room.

"Fuck you. And fuck your fame and power and all those things that make you Big Joey." Ella stormed into the room, determined to finish this argument with him.

"Sit down."

"Make me." She winced at the snide tone, closing her

eyes. She wouldn't win this argument by being a brat, but her head and stomach swirled and she was all off-balance from way too much wine. Joey's knees banged into her legs, and his arm hooked around her hip. Her eyes flashed open as he crash-tackled her onto the hotel bed. Her breath whooshed out of her, unable to scream 'what the fuck' at him.

"If I'm going to argue with you, let's do it at the same height." He lay beside her on the bed, their faces level, only an inch apart, his breath hot on her lips. Understanding sent blood rushing in her head, his proximity, and the frustration on his face warring inside her. There was only place that they were truly equal, here in bed. A little niggle told her she was too drunk to make a good decision now, but she batted it away. Fuck that. She wanted this. She wanted to disappear into passion with Joey. She'd already thrown away her career for him, why not enjoy the ride downhill on the way? It was what her mother did all the time.

She gripped his head and kissed him, fierce, throwing all her anger into the kiss. Wild energy crackled in the air. Enticing her. He battled back, rolling her underneath him as their tongues wrestled. Chemistry flowed between them, all that pent-up frustration, rushed as heat through her veins, back and forth as each fought for dominance in their kiss. Ella could barely breath with Joey's huge frame pressing her into the bed, and she wanted his weight. To die with his scent in her nostrils, all that masculine strength marking her demise. He lifted up on his elbows and she sucked in a deep breath, smelling only him, sweat, salted caramel, chocolate, the most sinful of desserts, and her own desperation added a bitter aftertaste.

"You want the famous guy. Here I am." Danger imbibed his voice. Ella ignored the warning sign and pushed against his chest. She ripped his shirt apart, buttons popping as her angry strength exposed his skin for her. Skin that she desired more than good sense. She slid her hands inside his destroyed shirt, shoving the fabric away as she reached for him. Her fingers hardly had a chance to explore before he rolled them sideways. Her hand went slack as he stripped her bare, shoving her bra down and exposing her nipples to the air. They were already hard for him, and she bit back a scream as his mouth covered one and sucked. Hard.

"I bet you are wet for me." He growled against her skin. A flush raced over her chest and face, and she could only whimper as he kissed down her stomach to her waistband. His hands surrounded her waist, and his torso covered hers. Her hands flew down to her pants and fumbled as she desperately tried to remove her clothes, as her hips rose up to meet his face. He pressed his tongue into her belly button, then shifted so his own hands were free. He covered her hands with his, and together they dragged her clothes off. Before she could take another breath, his head was between her legs, his chin pressing on her pubic bone as he drank her pleasure.

"Please, Joey." Ella begged him for his tongue, the weight of his body over hers keeping her hands hidden between them. She couldn't move, could only spread her legs wider, the muscles in her thighs taut with expectation as she lifted her hips up towards him and begged. Her body contracted around his tongue. He shoved it in deep inside her, without pause, giving her no moment to breathe. Pressure built and built and she clenched her hands at her sides, helpless under the onslaught of his mouth on her, and in her.

Then suddenly, he moved, leaving her empty as he lifted his face away from her.

"More, now. I need you."

"I have needs too." Joey's breath, hot and heavy, blew over her wet pussy and she pushed her hips up off the bed, trying to reach for him. Desperation, with her orgasm so close, had her writhing.

"Please." She pleaded. He answered in the best way possible. His tongue flicked over her clitoris and she ignited, coming in waves, her thighs shaking as all the evening's tension released. Her eyes fell closed, totally boneless, so sated she couldn't move. Joey slid off her, and her body followed him, slowly bending as she tried to wrap herself against him.

"Oh, no you don't." His fingers threaded through her hair, sharp tugs against her skull dragged out her of her devastation. "My precious Ella. You can't sleep now. You have work to do."

Her eyes flew open as his command reignited her previous self-righteous fury. Anger that he'd completely demolished with his clever tongue. Oh, God. She'd blown it down there at dinner, hadn't she? His comment about caring for her would've gone unnoticed if she hadn't grasped at it in drunken uncontrolled fury, spitting out her dreams for the world to hear. When would she ever learn?

"Don't you get tired of all the sycophants down there?" She waved her hand languidly. He caught it, staring at her with his brown eyes, darkened with desire.

"Only you could use a word like that while drunk and almost passed out on my bed."

She scrambled up, her head spinning as she sat up quickly, images of her mother in a drunken stupor on their couch rushing in her brain. She wouldn't become that; except she already was.

"All those people down there…" She blinked as she waved her arms, wild and loose, "they can fawn over you as much as they want, but I'm the one who gets to fuck you."

"You'd best get on with it, then." Joey's brown eyes glittered, narrow as his nostrils flared. She pushed his shoulders. He leaned back, his hands on the bed behind him, and his chest broad and open before her. The muscles on his chest and shoulders stretched taut and prominent, with his tattoo taunting her, tempting her, as it highlighted the strength in his shoulders. Ella straddled his legs, her fingers racing to undo his pants. His cock sprang free and she grabbed it with both hands.

"Settle down," he rasped. "We've got all night."

No, we don't. Her brain buzzed with a mix of heady over-indulgence and the remnants of way too much emotion. A frantic need to rush before she hit the wall, all her energy expended. She scrambled to push his pants out of her way, needing him inside her before an inevitable post-anger exhaustion won this battle.

"I have a condom in my chair." Joey's voice rumbled between them. "In the side pocket, well, you know where."

She paused, a dangerous voice inside wanting to say, fuck it, it doesn't matter, but common sense prevailed, just, and she shifted off the bed to stand up and grab the protection. Her panties caught on her ankles as she tried to take a step, and she landed back on the bed with an oomph. She stretched down and pulled her clothes off in a frenzied attack. Shoes, pants, the bra currently hanging around her waist, it all came off, hectic and wild. She reached for Joey's chair and slipped a condom out of the side pocket. As she twisted around to face him, his hands covered her waist.

"My beautiful Ella, a wild creature tamed only for me." He slid his hands up her sides and cupped her breasts. His touch seared her, sent shards of pleasure through her torso as his thumbs brushed over her tight nipples.

"Please." She gasped, trying to twist towards him. He kept her pinned against him, her arms helpless at her sides as his wrapped around her, toying with her.

"Please, what?" His teeth scrapped on her shoulder, and her fingers twitched. She wanted to drag her hair out of the way, expose her neck for him. Her head dropped backwards as he pinched her nipples, a moan escaping her throat.

"Please fill me." She pushed off the bed, using her momentum to twist in his arms, so her breasts pressed against his bulging chest muscles. He relaxed his hug as she traced his tattoo. Not slow and languid, but quick, rapid, his skin slick under her fingers, as she trailed them over the larger curling korus imprinted on his chest, then followed the line of hair down his abdomen to her real goal. His cock. She tore open the wrapper and rolled the latex over him. He groaned as she gripped him, her hand desperate as she stroked him.

He covered her hand with his. "Not now." He placed both their hands on her stomach, hers against her skin, and his huge hands stretched over her delicate hands. His fingers brushed the soft skin of her lower belly, sliding lower and lower until they grazed the edge of her pussy. Shivers of delight rushed over her. She needed him inside her. Now. She straddled him, throwing both her hands over his shoulders to grip his skull. She pulled his head towards hers, slamming her lips against his for a rough, rapid kiss. His fingers trailed down in her aching, wet softness. She cried out into his mouth as he pressed on her clit, her own hands digging harder against his scalp as pressure built, promising satisfaction. Soon. Not soon enough. Her body glowed, rich with need, making her skin alive. Tipsy with desire.

"Fill me."

He leaned forward. "No, you fuck me. Prove that you truly want this." There was a warning in his tone that she ignored. He pressed his body against hers, his hand squashed between them, inside her, as his other arm wrapped her tight. She tried to lift herself, to position herself so she could, but he held her tight.

"You have to let me move."

"Maybe I want you to fight for it." On every word, he moved his fingers inside her. She clenched around him, unable to think as he took her closer and closer to the edge. "Maybe I don't believe that you want me enough."

"I want you. I need you." Ella could hardly get the words out, her voice high and desperate. His fingers slid out and he relaxed his grip a fraction, keeping her surrounded and tight against him, sweat slick between them, but enough that she could push up on her knees. Enough for her to lift herself onto his cock. She sank onto him, impaling herself, not willing to wait another moment. He stretched her, hot and heavy inside. Perfect. She screamed as she came, convulsing around his cock.

"Keep moving." His hoarse whisper stopped her from collapsing, spent. He slid his hands on her waist in the rhythm he wanted, and she copied him. Riding his cock, moving for him, pumping herself on his hard length. Her thighs screamed with lactic acid, her knees ached as they pressed into the bed.

"Like this?" Desperation filled her voice. She was so close to another orgasm. Her legs started to shake, from working, and from desire.

"Faster." One command that she obeyed until she thought she couldn't move anymore.

"Please. Now." She needed him to finish as she pounded on him, her nipples dragging over his chest, faster and faster until he pulled her down onto him, shifting the angle slightly. He filled her completely, and she screamed as they came together. Hard inside her. She melted against him, collapsed, spreadeagled against his glorious body, panting in the aftermath. Her head rolled against his shoulder, and her eyes fluttered shut as the final shudders of her body twitched around him.

16

Joey gently rolled sideways, laying Ella on a pillow. She delighted him, so wild, spitting fury as she threw herself passionately at him. She was a demon in bed, and now, completely peaceful, as she slept in the aftermath. He brushed her tangled hair away from her face and hoped she wouldn't regret it in the morning. He'd made sure she knew what she wanted by asking her over and over. It would've been difficult to stop, but he would have at any point if she'd declared herself too drunk to consent. She'd only had one glass of wine at dinner; but her behaviour had been slightly erratic on the way to bed, and he'd wanted her to be sure of her choices. Her eyes flicked open and she smiled.

"I always wanted to know what whisky tastes like." The statement was gentle, none of her previous anger in her voice. Just a wistful longing for the unknown.

"It tastes like a burning flame on your tongue, soothed only by itself." Joey answered softly, hiding his feelings for her in the real truth of his words. Only she could alight him, only she could sooth the burn. He fell asleep with her in his arms, and in his heart.

The dawn light seeped through the hotel window. Joey tended to his morning ablutions, then slid back into bed, cuddled against Ella. Her breath stank, rank with last night's over-indulgence. He stroked her hair before turning away to snooze again. It didn't take long for the summer sun to wake up, streaming inside and onto the pillow.

Ella half-woke, groaning. "Holy hell, my mouth feels like it's full of cactus."

"But you only had one glass of white at dinner. All those years of abstaining has made you into a lightweight." Joey tried to joke. She cracked open one eye and peered at him.

"One glass?" Her face crinkled up, and Joey could see her hangover apparent in her expression.

"Yeah, it's a good thing I stopped you having that whisky, if this is what one glass of wine does to you."

"Oh, no." Her mouth dropped open and her eyes widened. "I had a whole bottle with Sal before dinner. Fuck me, what a fool I am." She dragged the pillow over her head. No wonder she felt so terrible then, going from never drinking to an entire bottle in one go. He reached out to his chair to grab the packet of paracetamol he always kept there.

"Have this—" His sentence was interrupted as she scrambled in the bed to sit upright.

"Sal. My friend, she had some bad news last night—" Ella rubbed her eyes, "—I'm so sorry to have to ask this, but her Nana is dying, and well…"

"I'm sorry to hear that."

"Me too. Nana is a great old bird, she always stood by me and Sal when times were tough."

"Then you are losing someone close to you too?"

"Yes. Very much so." Ella stared into the distance, her jaw clenched.

"We shouldn't have had sex last night if you were that drunk." A bitter taste coated his tongue; he didn't want to be that guy who took advantage.

She waved her hand. "I wanted that. I needed you… I mean, your cock and the release. Shit."

His heart swelled at her admission. "I'm glad I'm your safe place."

She rubbed her face. "Yeah. Look, I really don't want to ask you this."

"Ella, surely you know by now that you are special to me. If there is anything I can do to help, please let me know." Joey waited. Whatever Ella wanted, whatever support she needed, he would give her.

"You don't have to if you don't want."

"Spit it out." This prevaricating was starting to irritate him, especially before breakfast.

"It'd be really cool if you could come and say Hi to Nana… Sal's Nana in her last days. She's always been a huge league fan. Please."

Joey wrapped the hotel blanket in his fist, his knuckles white as rage flooded his body. Memories of Ella taunting him last night about his fame rushed back. Everything, all the feelings he had for her, they were all one-sided. She only wanted his fame, his name, to be seen with Big Joey. Fucking Ella. So much for being her safe space. He'd thought she was different to all the others, but no. All she wanted was to bask in his fame. She was right here asking if he'd do the whole famous guy thing for her, as if it were no big deal. The old grandma had probably never even watched a game, let alone know who the Tigers were.

Her face flushed with excitement at the prospect of introducing him to some random old lady. There was no disguising the way her eyes glowed right now. He'd really thought this could be something special between Ella and him. She'd seemed so interested in him, not his past glories, or his chair, or any other fucking thing. Somewhere in the last three weeks, this had progressed from great sex to an actual relationship. And now he discovered it was all a myth. She didn't truly want him, she just wanted his public persona, to hang off his fame. She'd probably announced their relationship to the committee last night on purpose. Had she faked being drunk last night, so he'd feel guilty today and do her bidding?

"I shouldn't have asked." Ella whispered fiercely at him.

He jerked his head up at her tone. "What do you mean?" Perhaps he'd over-reacted to her question?

"Maybe it's best if we have some space between us." She changed direction, and he frowned at her. Spots of pink appeared on her cheeks, her words tight as her nostrils flared.

"Maybe it is." Although, if he was right about her motivations, why would she ask for space? Wouldn't she want to stick with him? She kept her gaze on the window at the end of the room.

"If you wanted space from me, why did you ask me to

visit Sal's Nana?" he asked. He leant towards her, close enough to breath in her clean, vanilla scent. Fuck, he wanted Ella. All doubts about her reasons melted away whenever he was close to her, the old anger fading to a quiet pulse in the back of his neck. She sat, statue still, in bed next to him, completely nude apart from the blanket resting over her legs.

"That's for her, not for me." She spoke so quietly, he almost missed it, even though he was impossibly close to her. A murmur of white noise blossomed in his ears, maybe she didn't want him for his fame. Maybe he'd leapt to the wrong conclusion.

"What's the matter, Ella?" The heat between them burned so bright, it would be a shame to let it fade out after one tense morning. He had to know if he could fix this, whatever it was. Either that, or her nudity and proximity completely messed with his ability to rationalise anything, and she was a fame seeker who was also a bloody good actress.

"It's not you—" She paused, blinking one long slow blink. He sucked in a deep breath to quiet the confusing riot in his guts. Maybe he was right not to trust her motives. Especially if she could be swayed so easily.

She cleared her throat. "It's not you." A long deflating breath huffed out of her, and she sagged against the bedhead.

"What do you want, Ella?" He resisted the urge to scratch the back of his neck as the hair on his arms and the base of his skull rose.

"That's the problem, isn't it? I thought I knew." She tilted her head to stare at him, her mouth turned down at the corners. "And then you came into my life…. And now I don't know who I am anymore."

"Perhaps we should get dressed and have something to eat before we discuss this." Otherwise he would wrap her up in a hug to try and remove all this doubt from her life. He enjoyed bantering with her about how to approach different problems at her work, surely, they could talk about whatever was bothering her now.

"Back off, Joey. I don't want this intensity with you. I need to control my life, to know who I am and where I'm going." She leapt out of bed and scrambled around the hotel floor tugging on her scattered clothes. Maybe he should just let her leave? No, he had to finish this. He had to know the truth before it broke him.

"Ella." He sat up as tall as he could. "Come back to bed."

"Why?"

"So I can argue with you properly."

"I don't want to argue with you. We did enough of that last night. I have to fix the mess I made at dinner, and I don't need you to complicate things."

"Did you just admit that you announced us to everyone? That it wasn't my fault." He bit back the smile that threatened to undermine his annoyance with her.

"Not everything is about you. I came home yesterday, for the first time in weeks, to find out that someone special to me is dying. Yes, I may have had a little too much to drink. But you know what?" She leaned over and stabbed him in the chest with her finger. "It's not about you. I should have called Sal before yesterday. Instead, I'd spent all my time with you, abandoning her, my best friend. I should have known about Nana. I should have stayed with her last night. But no, I made the terrible mistake of going to dinner with you."

"It was a work dinner." Joey stared at her. Was she mad at him because she felt guilty about her friend?

"And what a disaster that turned out to be. Now everything thinks I'm screwing you…"

"You are."

"Yeah, but they, all of them, don't need to know."

"I don't see what the big deal is."

"Why not? I have a reputation to uphold. I've made the Exec team on sheer hard work and talent. Without ever using my body. But no one will see that. They'll all think I got there, the only female on the team, because I'm willing to fuck my way up."

"Does it matter what other people think?" This argument made no sense. One of the things he liked about Ella was that she didn't care what others thought of her. Had he misread everything about her? He rubbed the back of his neck.

"How can you ask that? All you care about is maintaining your reputation as famous Big Joey."

"No. That's all you care about." He'd been right. Damn it.

"Are you fucking kidding me?"

"No." He spoke quietly, a counter to her fury, unsure if he could trust her response.

"If you believe I'd stoop so low, if you are willing to think the worst of me, then fine. Visit Nana, do the famous thing, then fuck right out of my life." She swung of the bed and finished getting dressed. He transferred to his chair and threw his own clothes on. Together they went down in the lift, ate a hotel breakfast in silence, checked out, and left the hotel in silence, not even looking at each other. Joey spent the awkward hour concentrating on the small details of each task. Cutting his bacon into pieces. Sipping his coffee. Trying to decide if he should have another egg. Anything but look at Ella and lose this battle of wills between them.

"Where to?" He used the minimum of words, as he drove out of the hotel carpark.

"Ashfield." Silence descended again, only the steady thrum on the radio and the throb of his car's engine filling the space. They often drove in silence, a companionable silence in the mornings, while she sent emails and worked, and he drove. Today, the silence between them vibrated with unspoken fury. He gripped the steering wheel tight, staring stonily at the road, as he navigated the traffic, heading west. He couldn't speak to her. She only wanted him for his fame, so that is all she'd get. His face, his car, none of himself. All the way along Parramatta road until he turned onto Hume Highway at the edge of Ashfield, and with every turn, his heart continued to shrink. Why was he doing this for her? To absolutely prove his fears right.

"Where to now?" He'd never been one to hold a grudge or stay mad for too long, yet he growled at her. Simply asking her for directions created acidic bile in the back of his throat. She sniffed as he pulled up at the lights. He glanced over to see a single tear sitting at the corner of her eye. Shit. He was probably over-reacting about this, but it was the one thing that truly mattered to him. He wanted a true partner who saw him as himself, not as a wheelchair user, or as someone famous who could help their own career through proximity to him.

"She's in the rest home on Arthur St. Go along here, I'll show you where to turn left." She shook her head, and that little drop of fluid rolled down her cheek. He reached up and brushed it away with his thumb.

"I'm sorry about your friend's Nana, Ella."

Five minutes later, he parked on the street where Ella showed him. She leapt out of his car, almost as if she had panicked when he'd touch her, and couldn't wait to get away. There was still something she hadn't told him yet, something that mattered and he was at a loss to understand what was going on. If he didn't admire her strength so much, there was no way he'd be here. He heard the back door of his car thump shut and looked around to see her unfold his chair. She checked for traffic on the quiet suburban street, then walked around to his door with it.

"Thanks." He transferred into the chair, quickly rolling off the road.

"No problem. It's this way." She spoke as though they were strangers, even though she'd helped him without a second thought. It was that undercurrent of simplicity about him and his body that he really loved. Loved? No. Not when she was only here to parade him in front of people to fulfill her need for career advancement. He dragged in a deep breath, then blinked as he read the sign on the front wall of the rest home. The building was part Victorian villa, with intricate ironwork along the balcony, and part massive modern extension.

"Quong Tart's Gallop House?"

"Yeah. Ironic, isn't it. The old family home was sold a several generations ago. It's changed hands several times, and now it's been made into a rest home, they slapped old great-great-grandpa Quong's name on the front." Ella sounded relaxed, her usual self, for a moment. She walked towards the front door as if she came here all the time, only a slight pause as she entered the building, making him wonder if it was her first time here. The entrance had been widened to fit his chair and the path levelled so there was no step, a standard alteration for a rest home where they must wheel people about quite a lot. A broad hallway ran down the building with a reception window at the side near the door, with barely a trace of the old Victorian villa that Mr Tart had built nearly a hundred and fifty years before.

"We are here to see Mrs MacKenzie," Ella said to a neatly attired receptionist.

"Is she expecting you?"

"Yes." Joey couldn't hear any lie in Ella's voice, only her bold confidence that the world would do her bidding. That was the Ella that he adored. He wanted to reach for her, to sooth away the hurt that still hung around her shoulders. Hurt replicated in his own body, tense muscles wary of her change in motivations to be with him.

"This way." The receptionist stood up, walked out into the hallway to indicate the Ella should follow her. The receptionist sent a look towards Joey, seeming to him to see right past him. He rolled after them, his wheels silent on the tightly woven carpet. The building quickly changed into the modern section, and they followed the receptionist deep into the building along a bland hallway with many doors. Eventually, after turning a corner, she stopped and knocked on a door.

"Mrs MacKenzie, there is a visitor for you. Another one." The receptionist pushed the door open and stood aside. Ella walked in and held the door for him. Joey couldn't help but send a charming smile at the receptionist as she jerked in shock to see him roll past her.

"I'm with her." He'd met many hospital receptionists in his time, and this one fitted the mould of someone who resented her job. Only there for the measly cash, and not at all interested in the people who came through the door. Surely, a different job would be more appropriate, but then jobs weren't that easy to come by. He may as well smile and give her a little piece of happiness in her daily drudgery. He turned and focused his attention on the room.

"And who is this?" A wrinkled old lady sat in the bed, surrounded by pillows. She had that shrunken look of someone who'd been on this earth for many years, although her eyes sparkled with good humour in a face covered in wrinkles.

"Nana, this is Ella's—" A woman spoke from the far side of the bed, presumably Ella's friend, Sal.

"Hi, Sal." Ella shared a look with her friend, one that conveyed softness and care. She turned back to Nana and waved towards Joey. "This is Joey Mananui. He's a friend of mine. You remember him, Nana?" Ella's voice rang out, slightly too loud in that tiny room, as if she were forcing it.

Joey raised one eyebrow. Friend? He wanted to call bullshit on that comment. What they'd shared was a lot more than friendship, and given their current argument, he'd say friendship was somewhat overstating the matter.

"Yes. You are the cocky bastard who stole a premiership from my Dragons four years ago. I remember you." Nana pointed at him with a fragile, trembling finger, as she spoke like a true fan of the game, her passion colouring every syllable.

Joey grinned. "A team effort." All the doubt about this visit fled in the face of a real fan. Ironic. He wanted to be seen by Ella for more than his achievements on the field, yet he loved it when people loved his sport as much as he did.

"Nicely done, Mr Mananui. That storming try in the last ten to put your Tigers in front sealed the fate of my Dragons." Nana shook her head, as a smile tugged at Joey's face. The moment he'd burst through the line, ball in hand, with only a few metres of green grass between him and the crucial white line of paint he needed to step across to place the ball down and score. One of his finest moments, and favourite memories.

"I use that footage in the opening frame of my speeches."

"As you should, boy. You might have beaten my team, but I appreciate your style in doing it." Nana reached out with a thin hand. He rolled over and cradled the soft, fragile skin in his giant palm.

"I'm pleased to meet a true fan of the game." The tension in his shoulders started to fade. "It's a shame you support the wrong team."

Nana grinned and squeezed his hand. In her younger days, it would have been a fierce grip, today the squeeze was soft, gentle, only a remnant of the strength in her soul.

"You'll keep." The old bird winked at him. She turned her head, slowly, towards Ella, and he rolled backwards out of their way. Nana's hand slipped out of his.

"Now tell me, Ella, what type of friend is this Joey to you? A bland one, or one that might convince you that you can be more than a soulless lawyer?" Nana's eyes sparkled as she confronted Ella. Joey had to bite back a laugh, and from the other side of the room, her friend Sal coughed.

"Being competitive doesn't mean I'm soulless." Ella raised her chin defiantly.

"Winning legal arguments won't keep you warm at night," Nana said, and this time the chuckle did escape Joey's lips. Ella twisted quickly to glare at him, then turned back to Nana.

"Nana. It's complicated." Ella's tone screamed in warning.

Nana grinned. "Complicated as in he likes you more than you are ready for, or you like him and aren't sure what he feels. Oh, young love. It's a mess, and it's glorious."

Joey's whole body tensed, shimmering with anticipation for Ella's next words. She said nothing, and Nana spoke again into her silence.

"Don't be shy, Ella. You can tell your old Nana everything."

"Should I leave for a moment?" Joey skimmed his hands on his wheels, ready to roll out of the way.

"Oh no, Ella should be brave enough to tell me what she

thinks in front of you. I already know what she's going to say." Nana winked in his direction.

"Nana, you know my mother. You knew my father. Theirs was an intense love story, and after Baba died, you know what it did to Mama."

"You are not your mother, Ella. You have strength about you. You can face whatever the world throws at you. Your mother was always weak willed, even before her heart got broken in the accident." Nana spoke in the no bullshit fashion tone that only the elderly could get away with. Joey saw Ella swallow, her face drawn down in a frown. Was this the missing clue to her behaviour at dinner last night? The reason she was so upset at their relationship being announced to the public?

"Mama always followed her passions—first Baba, then a bottle. I won't be like her. I won't be led by my emotions." Ella stormed out of the room, her head held high, leaving only a zephyr of air that swirled around him as she left. Realisation hit Joey in the chest. Did Ella really equate the intense sexual chemistry between them with her mother's alcoholism? No wonder she set so many rules around their initial interactions, and why she ran away every time things got intense between them. He clenched his jaw; she was still running.

"I'll follow her," Sal said.

"No, Sal. Leave her," Nana said firmly. "How is Alicia getting on? Have you got a puppy yet?"

"Are you sure, Nana? Ella's pretty upset." Sal ignored Nana's attempt to shift the conversation, and Joey felt like an interloper, his gaze flicking back and forth between them.

"Chasing her—" Nana stared at them both, "—will only make her dig in her heels. She needs space to realise that she isn't her drunken mother. Love is tricky, and she's facing the prospect that a man loves her when she isn't ready for it."

Joey's eyes widened. "I do love her. I worried that she was only interested because of my past."

"Balderdash." Nana waved her hands. "I see the truth in the way you look at her. That scares her, and so it should."

Joey grinned, and the dryness in his mouth disappeared. "Why?"

"You'll expect her to rearrange her life for you. She doesn't want to do that." Nana's statement made Joey's head hurt. He would also have to change his life for Ella, that was the whole point of a relationship, a partnership. She couldn't keep him at a distance forever.

"I'm going to make sure she is okay." He rolled out of the room, down the hallway, giving the receptionist a little wave on the way past, until he zoomed outside. The summer air hit him in a rush that stole the air from his lungs. He rolled out onto the footpath, peering up and down the street to see nothing. Breathe, relax, this is her neighbourhood. She is sensible. She'll be fine. He pulled out his phone to see a message from her.

Ella: I need some space.

Joey: Are you okay?

After a moment with no reply, he pressed the screen to dial her. His phone dinged.

Ella: I'm at the library. Please leave me alone.

Joey slumped in his chair. Now what?

17

Ella woke up on Monday morning, and went through her daily routine like a robot. Time to face the music and apologise for overreacting at dinner on Friday night. She told herself that she felt nothing, no emotional response at the prospect of talking about it, and she was glad for the lack of feeling, after spending the last two evenings crying herself to sleep alone. From the first sip of wine with Sal, everything had gone wrong, and it was her fault.

She should never have asked Joey to flaunt his fame—no matter how great it was to see Nana smiling—it wasn't right to throw that expectation to perform at him. She flung her bag, her massive bag jerking at memories of her and Joey laughing at its size, across her shoulder, and let out a shuddery breath. Being away from him was the right thing to do. She had to leave for everyone's benefit. But why did it feel so wrong? Life was so unfair. This had started as a few fun evenings with better sex than she'd ever had, or ever would have again. She craved him, a physical hurt in the depth of her abdomen. If only the thought of being with him, of letting him into her life, didn't scare the pants off her.

Shit. She threw down the bag. She was scared. Scared that she chased a physical high like her mother chased the buzz of alcohol. Scared that she wouldn't be enough for him. Scared of being loved.

Shit. Fuck and balls. She'd screwed this up, before it had hardly started. She would have to fix it. She pulled out her laptop, opened Google Maps, and hunted for ages, looking for the right place before she sent Joey a text.

Ella: We need to chat. Meet you at 7pm Burnsey Park East.

She switched her phone to silent, not wanting to hear it ding if he responded, and chucked it into her bag. She swung the bag over her shoulder, this time smiling at the memory of him teasing her and went to work.

That evening, at ten to seven, with the sun still high in the bright blue sky, Ella smoothed out the tablecloth on the park table. Two paper plates, with bamboo cutlery sat neatly, and the food she'd prepared waited inside plastic containers to keep the insects off. She'd come here early to get the best table—overlooking his beloved ocean—with no guarantee Joey would arrive. She stared at her phone for the seventy-zillionth time. Still nothing further from him. That single 'maybe' he'd sent at lunchtime glared back at her, a mix of hope and despair. She put the phone in the back pocket of her jeans. Thank fuck for jeans and their pockets. Time stretched. Her leg jiggled as she sat staring at the ocean. The phone dinged, vibrating against her arse.

Joey: Where the fuck are you?

Ella: In the park. Where are you?

Joey: In the car park.

Ella: Coming.

She ran, her sandals slapping on her mostly bare feet as the grass crunched underneath. The crisp smell of summer drought, dry grass and dusty dirt, filled her nostrils as she sprinted. She skidded to a halt, scanning the carpark for that big green Mustang of his. Fuck. Nowhere.

Ella: I'm here. Where are you?

Joey: Here.

Panic spread in her veins, heavy in her chest, making her heart race and her skin freeze. She sucked in a deep breath and hit the call button. Her phone rang once before he picked up.

"What are you playing at?" His terse voice filled her ear. She waved her arm high above her head.

"I'm waving. Can you see me?"

"No. All I see is a few scrubby trees and a path with steps."

"Steps. That can't be right. I made sure the access was perfect."

"Well, it's fucking not." His tone made her pause.

"Where exactly are you?" Please don't be in the wrong place.

"Burnsey Park carpark."

"Burnsey Park East carpark?"

"What's the difference?"

"I don't know. Give me a second." She opened the Google maps app to look at where she was. The little blue dot sat at the edge of the carpark where she stood. She scanned the map. Oh, shit. The carpark curved around and had another entrance. How had she not seen that when she organised this?

"I'm done."

"No, wait. I've worked it out. There are two fucking carparks for this park." She dashed away a tear with the back of her hand. How could she screw this up so royally? An apology hovered on her tongue. She'd already messed up so much and she needed to make everything good between them again. Today was the day she'd stop being scared of love and embrace it. An odd noise from Joey stopped her and she swallowed, suddenly knowing how to fix this.

"Wait there. I'm coming to you. I'll be about—" she flicked to the map app and back to the call, "—about four minutes." She shoved the phone in her back pocket and raced back to the picnic table. She grabbed the tablecloth by the corners, folding everything into a sack, everything crashing together in her haste. She tossed it over her shoulder, and in the other hand, hoisted the small esky filled with two beers for him, a juice for her, some ice, and plenty of prawns. Scanning the park, she found the path to the other carpark, and rushed in the direction of Joey. She must look ridiculous, running down the path with her picnic slung over her shoulder. The food containers and plastic cups slapped into her back with every stride, a mocking hurt that would leave bruises. It didn't matter.

She had to fix everything. The path, thankfully, was short, and soon she stood at the top of four steps. Four steps. That's all it took to illustrate what a monumental cockup this was. Her lungs burned and her arms ached as she lugged the picnic down the stairs, taking her time to balance properly. It would be just her luck to sprain her ankle and sprawl on the ground while the picnic scattered everywhere. She let out a little sigh as she made it safely to the carpark and looked up.

There, all alone in the carpark, sat Joey's green Mustang. She stormed over to his driver's side door, her chest heaving with effort. His elbow hung out of the open window. She dropped the esky and shook out her hand, her fingers all sore from carrying it too tight.

"I'm sorry. I thought I had it all planned so it would be perfect. I searched for ages for a park where we could look over the ocean, you know, like you love about your house. I wanted a park that had a carpark with good access, one where you didn't have to roll too far. It was perfect." She babbled and with every word, tension ratcheted tighter in her chest. The tablecloth dug into her hand, the pain a physical reminder that she'd messed this all up. She could barely breath and her heart hurt from thumping so fast.

"Wouldn't it just shit you to tears!" Joey sounded like he was laughing. She peered inside to see him grinning at her.

"What?"

"I looked at your text. It says Burnsey Park Fast."

"Does it?" She put the tablecloth on the ground. It unravelled, exposing the mess of her picnic as it sprawled on the ground beside her. The lid had come off the papaya salad, the dressing seeping through the cloth, with the sharp scents of Thai mint and chilli adding a confusing note to the air. She pulled out her phone and scrolled back up her messages. Yeah, there it was. The error that caused this mess.

"Fucking autocorrect." She closed her eyes, her head bowed. Joey's laugh floated out the window of his car.

"Gotta love technology. Come and sit inside with me. Leave all that crap there."

She couldn't litter the carpark, so she collected the broken dreams of her perfect picnic apology and dumped them into the boot of his car. She walked around the car to the passenger side door, opened the door, and slipped into the seat. The cold air-conditioned air of his car swept over her sticky skin, cooling the sweat created by running while hefting a picnic under the Sydney summer sun. Joey put his huge, warm hand on her trembling thigh.

"I wasn't going to come. And when I got here and saw the steps, I nearly left."

"Why didn't you?" She twisted towards him.

"Because you've always had the right reactions to my chair. Seeing the stairs told me something was wrong. Not with you, or me. With the directions. I figured I'd punched them into Google wrong."

She nodded, unable to speak.

"I read your text again. I had the right place. And the 'fast' made sense. You are always in a rush."

She blinked back the hot tears that threatened. "I'm sorry. I can learn to be more patient. I'll slow down for you."

"No." Joey shook his head slowly. "Ella, please don't change. You are beautiful the way you are."

"Really?"

"Yes. And I don't want you to fear me." Joey stroked his hand down to her knee, a gentle touch that filled her chest with joy.

"I'm not scared of you. I'm scared of us." Her shoulders tensed as she hugged herself.

"Is that why you run away every time I get too close to you?"

Ella shook her head and let out a giant sigh that vibrated through the car. "How is it that you see me better than I see myself? Yes, I run away from this. What we have is so intense—" She swallowed away the dryness in her mouth.

"Ella…" Joey's tender rumble swept over her skin, a soothing sound. She sucked in a short breath, her shoulders starting to relax. How to explain this to him?

"I… ahh… I've spent three weeks with you. Lost to this passion between us, and I never do that. I'm not in control of this … whatever it is between us. For fuck's sake, I drank so much the other night, I behaved like… well, you were there. I never drink."

Joey nodded. "And that's why you had to run again?"

"Yes. But I ran right to you. I didn't truly freak out until then. I don't know if I can change that reaction." It had been so easy to blame her night of over-indulgence on Joey, as an extension of the excess passion she felt when with him. So easy to fall into the same old patterns of needing to control every little detail of her life, but that would mean no Joey. She loved him. All she needed to do was be brave enough to tell him. Her heart pounded in her chest, fast enough to make her ribcage ache.

"My sweet Ella, I love the way you attack the world, your drive for success, the way you don't let anyone stop you from your goals." Once more, he was braver than her.

She licked her dry lips. "What are you saying?" Maybe

she'd lain the blame in the wrong place, maybe it was purely the shock of hearing Sal's news about Nana that had culminated in one night of anomaly. Could she treat this relationship like any other goal, and stay and fight for it rather than leave when it got difficult?

"I'm saying that we can work it out. I can wait for you. Whenever you are ready."

"Part of me wants that to be now, but—" Ella swallowed. Was it possible to have a good overwhelming connection to someone? Could she step past her old need to stay calm and controlled? Like a flower bursting from the soil that previously held it steady and still, to bloom with Joey providing the sunshine necessary for success.

"I love your smart mouth. I love the way you are perfect for me."

"No one is perfect," she whispered. Hadn't she just proven that she was far from perfect?

"I didn't say that. I said you are perfect for me." His declaration should have come from her. She was the one who needed to fix what she'd broken between them. Oh. She felt lightheaded and flushed at the same time, an impossible rush of emotion echoed throughout her body as her blood pumped through her veins. She couldn't think, only feel the impossible joy as he said all the things she wanted to say. There was only one thing possible that she could do. She recited her speech. The one she had practiced for her failure of a picnic. The one where she declared her feelings for him.

"We met because I was a fan. I hoped for an autograph, and I ended up with so much more." Heat flushed over her face at the memory of their first night. "The person I idolised before we met isn't the real you, it was the public you, the version you let everyone see. Thank you for letting me meet the real you, to really see you." She paused. The speech sounded awkward, like a funeral eulogy. She cleared her throat and turned to look deep into his eyes. She placed her hands gently on his cheeks, the roughness of his stubble under her palms. "I love you, Joey. The real you, the one who makes me laugh, who doesn't deride me when my plans fail, who is spectacular in bed. I'm scared, but it's a good kind of scared."

"We can go slower if that's what you need."

Ella sighed, a fluttery, breathy sigh that turned into a laugh. "You know, I don't think we can."

"If it is what you need, we have to try."

A happiness settled over her, infusing her body all the way through. "I'm a mess, but you don't seem to mind. That's what I wanted to show you with today's picnic. How much you mean to me." She bit her bottom lip. "It didn't work out properly. I'm really sorry that I screwed up. I don't care about your fame. There's only one thing it was good for. Introducing me to you. I'm the luckiest person in all of Sydney and I nearly threw it away with a typo."

"It worked better than you could have hoped." Joey grinned that charming, cheeky smile that warmed her all the way through. She was a mess, a foolish conflicted person, to have questioned this chemistry—this love—between them.

"Really? I fucked it all up."

"Yeah. Nah. You didn't. Between your autocorrect and my google fail, it's something we'll laugh about together when we are old." Joey reached up to his own face and placed his hands over hers, a comforting connection to him. Her already heightened blood soared at his touch. She stretched towards him and pressed her lips against his. He tasted like home, like victory over her troubles, and she wanted this. She wanted to stop running from herself because she'd found the one place she could be free to be herself. The place where she loved, and was loved in return, regardless of all her faults.

"Shall we go home?"

"Yeah." The car tyres screeched as Joey reversed, spinning the car and headed home.

"Joey!" She squealed as the car's momentum thrust her back in her seat. "You just said you could go slower if that's what I need." With a scramble, she did up her seatbelt, but there was nothing stopping the grin that burst across her face.

"But you like it fast." His face lit up in a smile that made his eyes twinkle with desire, as his capable, strong hands controlled the throbbing power of his car. She nodded. Fast, powerful, just how she liked him. How they loved each other.

Ten minutes later, they drove into his garage and she leapt out of the car to grab his chair for him. He transferred across and chuckled at her eagerness.

"Come here to me." He commanded with his hands outstretched. She swept into his arms, cuddled against his chest, as he rolled them together into the lift and up, up to his bedroom.

"This is where I belong, here, next to your heart." Ella

whispered against his stubbled cheek, her hands resting on his chest.

"Right where you should be." He placed his thumb under her chin, tipping her head up towards his, and her mouth welcomed his kiss. She infused the kiss with all the love she felt for him. Their initial chemistry had nothing on this kiss; the first rush of their relationship, so desperate and hot, now combined with love to create perfection. A true partnership between them. She shifted against his muscular chest, familiar, and hers alone to claim. His hands slid into her hair, and she moaned, happiness mingling with desire in her veins. Wet need made her legs quiver, as he kissed her deep as if he could taste her soul, and he wanted to devour her, cherish her.

"Take me, Joey." She begged him, as electricity sparked between them, the throb between her legs becoming insistent. She'd been right, they couldn't go slow together. "Take me hard, strong, fast, just how I like it."

"Anything for you." His voice, a sinful promise made true, rumbled on her skin. She stood up, dragged her jeans and lacy panties down to her knees, exposing her pussy for him. He growled as he freed his cock for her, quickly rolling a condom on himself. Seeing him sit there, ready and hard for her, made her want to give him the one gift he craved. She spun around, flicking her long hair down her back, and eased herself down onto his cock.

"You know that's my favourite." His voice cracked as she claimed him, nudging her entrance with his hard length.

"I know. That's why it's perfect for today." She arched her back, her skin in flames as she rocked above him, inviting him to thrust deep. His hands dragged over her waist, then down to cradle her ass as she waited, awareness hovering.

"Fuck me, give me everything you can." Her smoky voice, hoarse with anticipation, pleaded with him.

"Everything I have is yours, and together—" His hands tightened around her bottom, "—together we will fuck." He pulled her down onto him, filling her deep to her very core, stretching her with his length. He kissed down the length of her neck, teeth scraping, until she screamed. Spasms of pleasure raced through her. Together, they moved, glory in their connection. All it took was one brush of his finger over her clit and pleasure coursed in her body until she was flying.

"Joey, I love you." She cried out the truth as the waves of passion soared to new heights. He wrapped his arms around her, cupped her breasts tight sending more sensation to her over-sensitised nipples. Her body arched, trembled, ached for him, as they pumped together, hard and fast. And just as she thought she couldn't take anymore, his hands slid into her hair, and he sucked the back of her neck as he came. She pinned herself against him, as he buried himself in her.

"My wild, beautiful, Ella. My love." His words meant everything, more than the pleasure he'd skilfully wrangled from her body. She relaxed back against him, her head on his shoulder, limp. Complete.

Several minutes later, when she could breathe again, she twisted to face him. "Only one thing could make this better. You never did write me that note."

He plucked his phone from one of the pockets in his

chair and started typing, showing her the screen as he thumbed the words.

Joey: For Ella, Love Joey. My bold girl in the lift.

She laughed as she read the words from the moment they'd first met. "Oh my god, Joey. Shut up and kiss me."

"As you wish."

AUTHOR NOTES

Ashfield (a suburb in inner west Sydney) was founded by the merchant Quong Tart. Everything about him in this book is true, including the statue, which is on Hercules Street. Ella is his fictional great-times a few-granddaughter. I hope I've done justice to Quong Tart's history and I'm proud to have lived in the suburb he founded.

Mananui is a Maori word that mean hope. When split into two words, Mana Nui, it means great power/respect. Mana is the concept that is similar to gravitas in English, a person has Mana when they are deeply respected by the community and the community grants them leadership and power. Nui means big. I chose this name for Joey because I love the combination of great strength/power/respect along with hope.

ALL BOOKS BY RENÉE DAHLIA

Thanks for reading OUT OF HER LEAGUE. I hope you enjoyed it.

If you'd like to know more about me, my books, or to connect with me online, you can visit my webpage www.reneedahlia.com and if you sign up to my newsletter, you can grab a free book Ode to the Banh Mi.

Twitter
https://twitter.com/dekabat
Facebook
https://www.facebook.com/reneedahliawriter/
Instagram
https://www.instagram.com/reneedahlia_author/

Reviews can help readers find books, and I am grateful for all honest reviews. Thank you for taking the time to let others know what you've read, and what you thought.

You've just read a book in my Kapow series. The other books in this series are:

1. Out of Her League (fm with bisexual characters)
2. Rekindled (ff) Short Story (also included as a bonus in Out of Her League)
3. His Buxom Beauty (fm)
4. Craving His Spotlight (mm)
5. Her Pregnant Rival (ff)

If you liked this book, here are my other books:

Contemporary Series: Farrellton Foster Family

1. Betrayed (fm)
2. Liability (ff)
3. Forbidden (fm with bisexual characters)

Contemporary Series: Merindah Park

1. Merindah Park (fm)
2. Making Her Mark (fm with bisexual heroine)
3. Two Hearts Healing (fm)
4. Racetrack Royalty (fm)

Contemporary Series: Rainbow Cove

1. His Christmas Pearl (fm)
2. His Christmas Pride Christmas 2020 (mm)

Contemporary Series: Homage

1. Ode to the Banh Mi (fm with bisexual heroine)
2. Uplift (ff with bisexual heroines). In the Only One Bed anthology.

Historical Series: Great War Ladies

1. Her Lady's Honor (ff)

Historical Series: Bluestockings

0.5 Ten Shipwrecked Books (fm with bisexual hero). In the 12 Rogues of Christmas anthology

1. To Charm a Bluestocking (fm with bisexual hero)
2. In Pursuit of a Bluestocking (fm)
3. The Heart of a Bluestocking (fm)

BONUS SHORT STORY: REKINDLED

FOR EVERYONE WHO WORKED (AND CONTINUES TO WORK)
TOWARDS MARRIAGE EQUALITY. THANK YOU.

Irony: working to ensure marriage equality while her own relationship fell apart.

SAL and ALICIA have been together for over a decade, but for the last six weeks, they've been distant with each other. When Sal gets news of an inheritance, she decides to leave. The letter begins a conversation they should have had six weeks ago.

When I wrote this short story in 2017, it was my first piece of queer fiction and an important part of my realisation that I'm bisexual. On 9 December 2017, in Australia, the Marriage Act of 1961 was updated to give everyone the right to marry. The Act now defines marriage as '*the union of two people to the exclusion of all others, voluntarily entered into for life*'. While I wrote this short story, the battle to gain this right was being fought in a very public space. I want to acknowledge everyone who has worked towards the goal of marriage equality; not just in 2017, but for the many years leading up to that moment. And I acknowledge those who continue to work in this space.

I acknowledge the Wangal people of the Eora Nation whose land this work was produced on. I pay my respects to Elders past and present.

REKINDLED

What was it Einstein said? If you've failed at something twenty times, the next time just proves you are a fool? Sal had had enough of being ignored, of being the domestic workhorse in her relationship with Alicia. Except she was chained here by a mortgage, and her own loyalty. There was a certain irony in working to ensure marriage equality while her own relationship fell apart.

Sal ripped open the crisp official looking envelope and slid out the letter. Holy fuck. She blinked, read it twice, then swayed on her feet. Her share of Nana's estate was bigger than her feisty Nana had hinted at. Grief punched her in the guts at the hole left behind by Nana's death. Several months hadn't dulled the pain. Maybe time would never help. Rationally, Nana couldn't have lived forever, but damn it, ninety-three seemed pretty bloody close. Nana's final gift would allow her to sell her share to Alicia and move out. A gift of freedom from the chains holding her back. It wasn't just the mortgage chaining her down. It was Alicia as well. They'd been together for a decade now, slowly drifting apart. How long had it been since they made love? When had their comfortable silence turned into judgement?

When she'd heard about Nana's cancer, she'd gone to her best friend, Ella, not to her lover. Alicia had come to the funeral and said all the right things. Perhaps it was only Sal that noticed Alicia's eyes stray, too often, to her phone during the service. When had Alicia's job become more important than them? Or more importantly, how long had Sal known that she was second best in Alicia's life? In the last six weeks, especially, Alicia had become terse, almost rude in her dismissal of Sal. It hurt more than a punch to the chest, the slow ripping out of her heart as Alicia's behaviour squeezed the love out of her until all that was left was a sodden, bloody mess on the pavement. Ugly, brutal, beyond repair.

Sal placed the letter on the kitchen counter, and looked around at the small city apartment they'd shared for so many years. She opened the dishwasher and started putting away last night's dishes out of habit. To leave Alicia terrified her, a lead weight inside her gut, but here she was, still chained to their kitchen, still doing all the work around the house. Cleaning had become a metaphor for the emotional work Sal did for their relationship. Sure, they'd mutually decided that Alicia's career as a doctor would bring in more income than Sal's work at the small gay rights charity ever could. The long hours of Alicia's work, and the emotional strain of her job, meant that Sal ended up with all the domestic tasks. Slowly Alicia stopped noticing, and the balance shifted until Sal buckled under the burden. Chained to the house, and to this life, without any of the joy they used to have. And that's without the emotional load of the stupid postal vote, having to prove to the country that her love was equal to anyone else. Irony was the word of the day. She spent her days working so other people could shout their love in public, while her own dissipated in a pathetic slow demise.

She put away the lone wine glass, and single plate from the dinner she'd eaten alone last night. A tear dripped off her chin, splashing onto the counter. Sal sniffed, wiping her face with the back of her hand. Leaving would be hard, a guarantee that her heart would break. Maybe it was already broken, and that's why Nana's gift meant more than money. It was freedom to begin again. To find herself again.

A thump from the hallway made Sal jump. Oh, Alicia was home. She sucked in a long deep breath, ready to battle for her new life. The breath came out again in a big whoosh. That's why this was the right decision. Because talking to Alicia about anything real had become a battle.

"Are you home?" Alicia's dulcet voice called out. *Yeah, I'm always bloody home.*

"In the kitchen." Sal grabbed the letter from Nana's lawyer, clutching it to her chest. Alicia walked in, her hips swaying slightly as she casually approached Sal. Sal tensed as Alicia pressed a perfunctory welcome kiss to her cheek. The crisp, clinical smell of the hospital, with that undercurrent of Alicia's favourite jasmine perfume surrounded Sal. Only the crinkle of the letter between them, and the aching tension at the back of her neck kept her focused on the ugly necessity facing her.

Sal cleared her throat. "Doll, we need to talk."

"Can I wait? I had a shit day at work and would love nothing more than a glass of wine. Did you cook anything for dinner?" Alicia's dismissal sealed her fate.

"No, I didn't fucking cook anything for you. Why should I when you are hardly ever here?"

"What's the matter? Where is this—" Alicia waved her hand and the dismissive motion cut the thick air. "—coming from?"

Sal stepped away, her back hitting the bench as she tried to give herself space in their tiny kitchen. She waved the lawyer's letter between them.

"What's that?" Alicia's fine eyebrows arched up.

"I'm leaving. This is enough money to buy you out of this house. I'm done." The words came out easier than Sal imagined. They hovered between them in a pause that felt perfectly right. Alicia's mouth dropped open, deep furrows between her eyes.

"But… But, you can't."

"Yes, I can. I'm tired of being your servant, Alicia."

"What? That's not true. Where is this coming from?" Alicia's confusion had to be faked. Surely she knew.

"Seriously? Do you even see me anymore? No. It's just waltz in here. Fuck my job is hard. Give me wine and food. Clean the house. Do all the fucking work. Bear the emotional load of my own job without any support from you. Have you any idea how hard it is to read the news and see people fighting to prove that our love isn't real? That some fucking sky fairy God and his ideas matter more than the real people here on earth. And then you have the…" Sal hiccupped on a short breath. "… the gall to act surprised when I want to leave. This arrangement doesn't work for me anymore. I won't be your little kept woman doing all the shit work so you can have your dream career. What do I get? Prune hands from cleaning the bathroom, and lonely dinners. Eating alone in this perfect little apartment, waiting for you to grace my presence. I'm done." Sal pushed past Alicia and rushed into their bedroom. She grabbed the suitcase from the bottom of their wardrobe and started throwing her clothes into it.

"Wait. There is no need to be so extreme. Can't we talk about this?"

"I've tried, Alicia. I won't be your dogsbody, your PA, anymore." Sal grabbed handfuls of her shirts and stuffed them into the suitcase. Her favourite shirt, a birthday present from Alicia four years ago, peeked out. She tugged at it until it came free. She balled it up in her fist and flung it across the room. Alicia's arms surrounded her. Sal spun around in the embrace.

"You just don't get it, do you? This can't be fixed with a hug. Or sex. And fuck, how long is it since you even bothered to kiss me properly. When did we last have sex?" Fury made Sal's blood pump, her heartbeat erratic as she stood with Alicia's arms gently around her waist.

"I know it's been hard lately. Work has been crazy. I'm sorry I've ignored you."

"Alicia. It's not just lately. It's been ages. Months, years, even."

"But we agreed that it made sense to live like this."

"Years ago, Alicia. We agree that years ago. We've never talked about it ever again. You just take all the advantage of having a wife without asking me if I still want the role. Well, here's some news for you. I don't want this life anymore. I can't do all the housework for a stranger. I may as well go and get a job cleaning random people's houses."

"Why didn't you say something earlier? I don't want you to feel like this. What can we do?"

"It's too late for that…" Sal lifted Alicia's hands off her hips and sunk down onto the bed with her head in her hands. "Look, this doesn't have to be difficult. Nana, bless her, left me some money. I'll just buy out my half of this place and leave."

"Fuck." Alicia drew out the word on one long syllable. "You actually mean it."

Sal's head jerked up and she glared. "Of course I mean it. This isn't just an emotional little tantrum. I've been chained to you forever, and I need freedom."

"Freedom from me?" Hurt infused Alicia's voice, and she spread her hands over her chest and throat. Sal's chest tightened. What she needed was freedom from the drudgery of her life. Less support role, and more time to pursue her own dreams. Being surrounded by happy, hopeful couples at work every day gave her such a stark view of her own miserable relationship. She'd made so many other people happy with her work at the charity. It just didn't translate in her own life. All that happiness – and even though they'd got a vote for yes; 60% was goddamned too tight – added insult to her own shitsville relationship. Supporting without support. She shook her head slowly.

"Maybe it's unfair to spring this on you, but then, maybe it's unfair on me that my unhappiness is a surprise to you." Sal hung her head, eyes closed. After several minutes of silence, she looked up to see… nothing. Alicia had left. Typical. As soon as things got hard, Alicia upped stumps, and left Sal to do all the emotional heavy lifting. Sal stood up on weak legs and finished packing her suitcase. She zipped it shut, and walked out of their bedroom without another glance, dragging the case behind her.

Alicia stood in front of the door, blocking her exit. Sal raised her eyebrows.

"I've just quit my job." Alicia's eyes were wide and her mouth pinched at the corners.

Sal shifted from one foot to the other. She pressed the heel of her hand against her forehead because her head started to ache. "What?"

"My job. I hate it. I hate my boss. I was only doing it for you, for us, because I thought that's what you wanted."

"Hold on. But you love that job?" Sal staggered back a step and scratched the back of her neck. She abandoned the suitcase and walked aimlessly into the lounge. Her breath panted rapidly, as she turned back to Alicia. Alicia stood quietly, biting her lower lip.

"I thought you loved that job?" Sal's whisper echoed through their tiny apartment. And the unsteady beat of her heart became the only sound she could hear.

"Yes and no. I love being a doctor. But this job. No. I felt chained to it, because of you. I was doing it every day for you." The simple truth in Alicia's voice beat strong, drowning the flutter in Sal's stomach.

"I think we need to talk."

Alicia nodded slowly. "It's my fault. We should have

talked more before it came to this. I assumed you were happy, that you needed me to keep going, because the money I earned allowed you to make real change. You say my work is important. I say your work is more important. How many people have you made happy through your work?"

"And I assumed you loved your job, and it was more important than me." Hot prickles formed behind Sal's eyes.

"Nothing is more important to me than you. You are my everything. I'm so sorry that I got lost, chained to old thoughts, old assumptions."

"I…" Sal rubbed the back of her neck, "I can't believe you quit your job for me."

"My boss is a dickhead, a misogynistic twit. I didn't say anything because I didn't want to burden you with the worry. I thought you wanted me to be happy, so I couldn't tell you that I wasn't."

"It sounds very convenient." Sal spoke slowly, needing to draw out this rapid change. Unsure if she could trust this. Did Alicia truly quit for her? Or was this some sort of gaslighting nonsense, so that she would stay? Alicia sat with her hands folded calm in her lap, her wide eyes staring openly, patient.

"Tell me the truth, Alicia." Sal rubbed her arm.

"I know this last year has been awful, with the vote and all. And I didn't want to add to your burden. I hated seeing the dismay in your eyes after work each day, the same way our friends fought and complained and cried. Why should we have to fight to be seen as equal?"

"Preaching to the converted." Sal couldn't help imbibe

her voice with sarcasm. She folded her arms over her chest and glared.

"Eight months ago, David quit. He got a better opportunity, and a new boss was hired. I probably mentioned him, Dr Fornsley-Smith. You know, I don't even know his first name. He thinks he's above the rest of us ER doctors. He issues commands, he's not part of the team, not like David was. And worst of all—"

Sal leaned forward, unable to fight her attraction to Alicia as she talked. She'd always been a sucker for Alicia's stories. A decade ago, she'd fallen in love with Alicia and her steady way of seeing people. She was an amazing doctor because she listened, she had empathy, and she tried her best to understand the biases in the system. It wouldn't take much for Sal's heart to spill over with love again.

"Yeah, doll, what?"

"He found out about us six weeks ago. I've had a never-ending stream of 'all you need a good fuck, that'll cure you' since." Alicia's eyes glittered, awash with unspilled tears, her frustration apparent in her voice.

"Let me guess. He suggested his dick would be the ultimate cure." The fight inside Sal ebbed away, the rage in her veins slowing to a steady hum focused on Alicia's shithead boss, and on every other bigot who filled the world with hatred.

Alicia nodded slowly. "I know it's an easy harassment case, but I thought you wanted me to keep this job, that we needed my pay for the mortgage, so that you could keep doing the actual important work."

"So you said nothing. Not even to me." Hurt filled Sal's

chest until it ached more than she thought she could sustain. "Not even to me." She pressed her palm into her chest, hard against her heart. How like Alicia to think she was doing the right thing, and somehow she ended up doing the absolutely wrong thing.

"I didn't want to burden you."

Sal sighed, and her breath fluttered over her lips. "I want your burdens, Alicia. That's the entire point of a relationship. We share stuff that sucks before it gets to this point."

A muscle in Alicia's jaw tightened, and Sal imagined yet more unsaid words. She opened her mouth to protest when Alicia kissed her. The barest brush of soft lips together, so faint a touch that Sal wondered if she'd dreamed it. The hum of anger in her body switched into a throb of need. It had never taken much for Alicia to do this to her. She fucking loved the way Alicia kissed. Always had. That's partly why drumming up the courage to leave had been so difficult.

Her libido roared to life, sparks flying, wonderful and electric. Sal threw herself into the kiss, using her frustrations to turn it brutal, a clash of lips, teeth, tongues, a desperate grasp at the love they'd once had. Alicia, her perfectly imperfect Alicia, took it all, all her anger and lust and worry, and made it beautiful. Electricity zinged inside her core as they battled for their past, and maybe, just maybe, for their future. Alicia's hands threaded into her hair, sharp tugs on her skull as Alicia's hands made light work of her pony tail. Their kiss gentled as Alicia stroked her hair, long strokes over her scalp, her hands in a motion that should have been soothing, instead made Sal pant with need.

"Oh my God, Sal." Alicia whispered frantically against

her neck, as she kissed down her throat, along her collarbone. Sal arched against her, her hands slack at her sides under Alicia's caress. Sal licked her lips, every last furious fibre in her body now buzzing with arousal, as she stripped off her shirt. Her breasts, nipples tight, rubbed against her lacy bra as she pressed herself against Alicia's doctor's scrubs. Alicia pulled down her bra, exposing her nipples to the sultry summer air simmering between them. Sal whimpered as Alicia covered one breast with her mouth, warm and wet on her skin, heat and tension building in her core.

"More. I need more." Sal's voice turned smoky.

Alicia glanced up. "Be a good wife and wait." A fresh surge of fury buzzed in her veins at the comment, but Alicia's mouth returned to her breasts, pleasuring and punishing each in turn, until Sal writhed underneath her as unspent desire built and built.

"I am a good—" Sal tried to suck in enough breath to finish her sentence as Alicia tormented her nerves, sending pleasure spinning deep inside her. She was wet and ready. And, damn it, she was the perfect wife. Wasn't that both the problem and solution? She let out a shuddering breath, "—wife." Sal breathed in Alicia's jasmine shampoo, as her hair stretched out over her skin, spread by Alicia's steady drift southwards. Her kisses trailed around her belly button, and Sal cradled Alicia's head in her hands.

"Take off your pants." Only the throaty huskiness of Alicia's voice undermined the command, and Sal revelled in the knowledge that Alicia needed this release as much as she did.

Sal issued a command of her own, as the crisp fabric of Alicia's scrubs roughened her skin. "You take yours off."

"Not yet, my love." Alicia's declaration hit Sal like a pulse, and she came. Her hips bucking up against Alicia, who slid up her body to drink in her cries in a perfect kiss. A comforting kiss, familiar, yet fresh and new, infused with love and apology. Oh, thank fuck for small mercies. It'd been so long since she'd orgasmed, she'd wondered if she'd forgotten how. It only took a few touches from Alicia, and her body knew what to do, knew how to respond. Sal's hands clawed all over Alicia's back, stripping her clothes off, until she ran her hands down over Alicia's gorgeous heart shaped arse. Her palms against Alicia's bare skin, her fingers seeking out Alicia's lacy g-string, and following the promise down between her legs.

"Sal."

"Say please. If you want me to finger fuck you, you have to ask." Sal's fingers trembled as Alicia spread her legs wider, her thighs shaking with need.

"Please. I want you more than anything. I always have." Alicia's cry was hoarse, her eyes wide, and her lips parted. Sal drew circles on Alicia's arse, teasing her closer and closer to heaven, until Alicia's teeth scraped on her neck in desperation. Sal slid her fingers into Alicia's wet slit, her own skin alive with desire as Alicia cried out her name. Together they rolled on the couch, to lie face to face, mouths on each other, as they slipped fingers into each other's bodies, thumbs against each other's clits. Both of Alicia's hands toyed with Sal until she couldn't breathe, her heart raced with need and delightful, amazing pressure built in her core.

Alicia pinched Sal's clit and she groaned into Alicia's mouth. Alicia brought her wet thumb up to her own mouth, licking Sal's musk, their mouths so close, the scent overtook Sal's senses.

"God, Alicia, you'll be the death of me."

"Till death do us part." And on Alicia's fateful words, they came together, bodies pressed tightly against each other, so Sal couldn't tell where she ended and Alicia began.

Sal snoozed against Alicia, her head nestled against Alicia's shoulder.

Alicia's pulse beat strong against her cheek, and eventually, Alicia rolled so they stared at each other. "I'm sorry, Sal. I wanted to be so strong for you."

"Strength isn't keeping it all inside. Strength is being part of a team. Our team."

Alicia stretched beside her. "I guess I got lost somewhere."

Sal hummed an uncertain note. Should she forgive Alicia so quickly? Her frustrations had built over a long time, and here she was, ready to forgive after only a few vague comments from Alicia. Oh, and the best fucking set of orgasms she'd had in forever. She wasn't weak for believing Alicia. They had been partners for a long time; Sal believed Alicia. All was forgiven because…

"Oh my God, darling. I can't believe you quit your job!" Sal grabbed Alicia's cheeks, cradling her face with her hands.

"It had to be done."

"But it's so extreme—"

Alicia smiled, her gaze firmly on Sal. "Only a big gesture would be believable."

"What are you saying?"

"Sal, we've been together for over a decade, most of those have been the happiest years of my life. I want more."

"Mine too. My heart was in pieces knowing that my only hope for survival was to leave you."

"How could it come to that?"

"Think about it. All day at work, I'm surrounded by happy couples. Couples anxious to work together for a vote in their favour. And I'd come home to dinner alone while you worked crazy hours in a job you loved. It was so easy to measure us against them and come up wanting." Sal scratched the back of her neck, and Alicia gently tugged her hand to her mouth and kissed it.

"I did it for you, and I quit for you. It's always been for you, Sal."

Sal's breath hitched in the back of her throat, the truth in Alicia's words so very precious to her. Alicia brushed her fingers across Sal's cheek, wiping away the sole tear.

"But what do I do with Nana's money now?" Sal realised she didn't want to leave, the idea of splitting from Alicia had come from a desperate need for recognition, and she'd misread the whole situation. She blamed Alicia for not talking, yet she was just as guilty of the same problem.

Alicia grinned. "It's your money, do what you want."

"With you?" If they were to be a team, they could make this decision together.

"I would like that. Call it phase two of our relationship, where I learn to be a better wife to you."

"You want to be my wife?"

"Of course. Why would I spend so many years

supporting your work at the charity? You must know I worked in an unforgiving environment with a terrible boss so you could change the law, and I could finally tell the world how much you mean to me."

"Really?"

"Yes, really. You mean everything, Sal. Everything."

"Let's get married, doll." Sal smiled. They could discuss all their issues, and what to do next, as they planned together.

"Wait here. I've been waiting for this moment." Alicia leapt up and pulled open a drawer under the coffee table. She reached far into the back and pulled out a little box. Sal sucked in a shuddery emotional breath. How long had it been there? And how hadn't she seen it? Sal wiped her eyes with the back of her hand.

"Will you marry me?" Alicia opened the box, and showed Sal two perfect rings, made from tiny chains.

"Chains?" Sal's hands shook with overwhelming emotion. Getting married was everything, the whole reason she fought so hard at work, the whole reason she'd hated their drift apart. They'd seemed so close to being the perfect couple, and having the perfect life, and yet, it had all started to fade. Except it hadn't. They'd just forgotten to talk to each other. Sal had made the same assumptions Alicia made.

"Yes. Please say yes. I love you. I want to be chained to you forever." Alicia pleaded her case with one finger tracing Sal's cheek affectionately.

"Yes. I love you."

* 9 7 8 0 6 4 8 9 6 2 6 0 1 *